GOOD GIRL
SEEKS
BAD RIDER

GOOD GIRL
SEEKS
BAD RIDER

VONNA HARPER

LENA MATTHEWS

RUTH D. KERCE

POCKET BOOKS
NEW YORK   LONDON   TORONTO   SYDNEY

Pocket Books
A Division of Simon & Schuster, Inc.
1230 Avenue of the Americas
New York, NY 10020

First Pocket Books trade paperback edition March 2008

POCKET and colophon are registered trademarks of Simon & Schuster, Inc.

For information about special discounts for bulk purchases, please contact Simon & Schuster Special Sales at 1-800-456-6798 or business@simonandschuster.com

Manufactured in the United States of America

10 9 8 7 6 5 4 3 2 1

Library of Congress Cataloging-in-Publication Data

Good girl seeks bad rider / Vonna Harper, Lena Matthews, Ruth D. Kerce.—
1st Pocket Books trade pbk. ed.
    p.   cm.   (Ellora's Cave anthologies)
  1. Erotic stories, American. I. Harper, Vonna. II. Matthews, Lena. III. Kerce, Ruth D.
 PS648.E7G65 2008
 813'.60803538—dc22   2007047547

ISBN-13: 978-1-4165-7669-3
ISBN-10:   1-4165-7669-X

CONTENTS

VIRGIN
AFTERNOON

VONNA HARPER

ONE

*H*OW STRANGE IT WAS to see a man in her garage, but if any man had a right to be there, it was Bryan Aster.

"Are you sure, Lara?" he asked, with his head under the pickup's raised hood. "It's in great shape. And with that low mileage, you could get several thousand more than I can pay you."

"I don't need it, and Spence wanted you to have it."

Bryan's big, rough fingers continued to grip the top of the hood, but she doubted if he was still looking at the truck's inner workings. Being this close to her husband's best friend was disconcerting in ways she didn't want to hold up to the light. Part of her wanted him to leave, but she'd spent so much time alone since Spence's death—and even before. It was time to rejoin the land of the living and who better with than a man she'd known at least ten years?

"So you're going to move, are you?" He slammed the hood, rattling her nerves even more than they already were.

"I have to. I didn't tell Spence this, but it's in foreclosure. With the medical bills and his not being able to work and my having to take so much time off— What's that look about?"

Bryan shrugged, the gesture taking her back to when they'd all been in college and he had held down the catcher's position on the school's baseball team during that incredible year when the team had won the state championship. "I wish you'd told me."

"Why?" She tried a mischievous smile, something she hadn't felt like doing in too long. "You been robbing banks and are now giving away your ill-gotten gains? Even if you were rich, I wouldn't want anything. I don't want to live here anymore."

Lifted eyebrows served as Bryan's response. How healthy he looked, tanned with a full head of dark hair, the faintest shadow of lines around his eyes and at the corners of his mouth. Funny, she'd never noticed that small dark mole on his right cheek, but maybe she'd never studied him like this before. Hadn't felt his energy before. "Do you think I should stay?" she asked.

"I want you to do what you want to, Lara. You're the only one who knows what's right."

Lara. Damn, why did the sound of her name coming from his lips make her nerves jump? "I'm still relearning what I want. Look, it's hot in here, and there's beer in the fridge."

"There is? I didn't think Spence was doing any drinking near the end."

"He wasn't. This is left over from one of the last times you came to see him. He asked me to pick up some."

Again, Bryan let silence do its work. He led the way back into the house, his movements as familiar as if he lived here. He didn't of course because he and Carol had a condo some two miles away, but he'd been here countless times and probably knew the place's creaks and groans as well as she did. Taking two beers out of the refrigerator, he popped the lid on one and handed it to her.

"I don't—" she started, unable to take her eyes off his hand.

"Today you do. Come on, you always said you'd stoop to a beer if the day was hot enough. It's hot."

Yes, she acknowledged as they wandered into the air-conditioned living room and plunked themselves into adjacent recliners, summer had indeed arrived while she was too busy with the business of dying to pay attention. After briefly holding the can against her cheek, she took a sip. Wonderful!

His form filled the chair, shoulders scrunched a little to accommodate the inadequate space. Although he hadn't crouched behind home plate for years, he still carried himself as if he belonged there protecting his turf, battling for a win, daring a runner to knock him down.

"So," Bryan said, "do you know where you'll be moving to?"

"Not really. There's a fairly new apartment complex near work but after having my own house—so much adjustment."

Once again Bryan didn't immediately respond. Had he always been like this around her, not quite comfortable? Or was she a painful reminder of the good friend he'd lost?

"You look tired," he said.

"Bryan, Bryan, don't you know men aren't supposed to say that to women? It's hardly a compliment. Besides, you're the one who looks tired."

"Hmm. You didn't get much sleep near the end, did you?"

"I'm making up for it now. In fact, I can't seem to get enough."

"Because you were neglecting yourself taking care of him."

"What choice did I have?" Shocked by her sharp tone, she leaned forward. When she took a breath, she caught a hint of male heat. "I'm sorry. I swore I wouldn't whine, and I wouldn't have wanted it any other way. When Spence decided to go off the chemo, I knew it wouldn't take long. Being there for him was something I had to do."

"You're an incredible woman."

No, she wasn't. What about the nights she'd spent beside Spence's bed wanting him to die so the inevitable would be over? What about the insane anger that swamped her every time she thought about the damn cigarettes that had started everything? Or thought about Spence's increasing dependence on her, his disinterest whenever she tried to tell him what was going on at work, or in the world, or with their finances?

"What?" Bryan asked.

Blinking, she brought the room, or more specifically him, back into focus. Lordy, but that T-shirt was tight! And the shadow of a beard over a strong male bone structure only added to her agitation. "Nothing. Just a moment of that self-pity I'm trying to outrun. It isn't getting me anywhere. So, how are things going for you and Carol? I don't remember seeing her at the funeral, but then, that day was pretty much a blur for me."

"I'm sure it was. Look, about the mortgage here. Do they know what you've been through? Maybe they'll give you some more time to work things out."

"They know, and they've been patient, but this is honestly what I want. Ah, about the truck. Do you mind waiting to take it until after I've moved? It'll make hauling things easier."

He'd been studying the beer can as if it was the most interesting thing in the room, but now he met her gaze with his beautiful deep blue eyes. "You know the answer to that."

Yes, she did. Bryan had always struck her as a giving man. She'd never seen so much as a hint of selfishness in him. If anything, he went too far to put others before himself, particularly Carol, who was more than a little self-absorbed.

"Just say when," he continued, "and I'll round up some guys and we'll do the actual moving. As long as you keep the instructions simple, we shouldn't make too much of a mess."

"Thank you." Laughing at his lighthearted approach, she pointed at a box near the TV. "I've started packing up some of the small stuff. You tell me, what am I going to do with all those tapes now that everything is DVD?"

"Get rid of them, unless there's a sentimental attachment."

Sentimental was hardly the word she'd use. She shouldn't have drawn his attention to that particular box. Good grief, what would he think if he read the titles? Bringing the beer to her lips, she took another swallow. "You're right. This does taste good."

"Hopefully it'll help you relax."

She stuck out her legs, then frowned because she couldn't remember when she'd last shaved them. And thanks to the old shorts, she had to admit her thighs were downright scrawny. All these years of watching her weight and now she'd gone and lost who knew how many pounds without being aware of it. When she looked up again, Bryan was studying not just her bare legs but everything about her, it seemed. Something *zinged* in her, a hot, crawling sensation. "What?"

"Sorry. I just . . . do you feel all right?"

"This, you mean?" She flattened a hand over her scrawny thigh. "Give me a little time. I'm sure I'll fill out again. That's something I've never had a problem doing."

"Starting tonight. I'm taking you out for dinner."

"You don't have—"

"Not have to, want to."

The heat she didn't know what to do about became more intense, and although it might be less of a kick in the belly if she wasn't looking at him, she didn't drop her gaze. Reality 101—Bryan was turning her on.

Are you surprised? When's the last time you had sex?

Months, maybe a year. It wasn't that she hadn't thought about sex, far from it, but wanting and being able hadn't lived on the same planet.

"I, ah, thank you. What about the Roadhouse? The four of us used to love going there. Do you want to call Carol and—"

"She won't be joining us."

At his tone, awareness of Bryan as a man tamped down a little. This wasn't about Carol working late or having another obligation. He was trying to tell her something important but didn't know how to do it. "Why not?"

Bryan rolled his can between his palms. Like her, he was leaning forward, the lines at the corners of his eyes and mouth more prominent than they'd been a few minutes before. "We've separated."

Although she'd suspected them, the simple words rendered her mute. She ached to walk over to him and hug him but didn't dare. And that ill-defined heat was returning, distracting her. "I'm sorry, so sorry."

"So am I. I didn't want to dump this on you. You have enough—"

"You're my friend. I'm sorry I didn't know about this before."

He took another drink, then went back to rolling the can. "You couldn't have done anything about it, just as I couldn't make Spence well."

His truth hung between them. Had they once been fresh out of their teens with youth's optimism and ignorance and nothing to worry about except college grades and finances? Back then, those two realities had seemed pretty heavy, but in retrospect it had been nothing. "You're right. Do you want to talk about it?"

"Talk? No."

She'd expected that. After all, she and Bryan hadn't had one of those bare-your-soul conversations. Funny, she'd never thought about that before, but then she'd never been more aware of him than she was at this moment. "Something you said—Carol didn't come to the funeral, did she?"

"No. Not because she didn't care, but she knew I'd be there."

"How complicated things become. Are you all right?"

He'd gone back to staring at her in that way that made her feel alive. The reclusive creature she'd turned into wanted to jump, to run out of the room and head for safety, whatever that was, but the man-woman energy she was experiencing had to be dealt with, either by relegating it to the *are you insane* file or—or what?

"Yeah," he said. "I am all right. There've been problems be-tween us for quite a while. The point came when neither of us could ignore them anymore."

"She's ambitious." Was that better than saying selfish?

"So am I, but I don't understand why her career has to come before and instead of children."

Something new lived in Bryan's eyes, a vulnerability she'd never seen. He was no longer the jock who lived and breathed his sport and thought success rode on his batting average. Now, like her, he lived in the real world. Studying him, she mentally placed a baby in those big hands. Instead of looking awkward and uncomfortable, his hands knew how to cradle and comfort. "I know you want children."

"I have for years. I want to coach my son or daughter's team no matter what sports they play, among a million other things."

"Ah, Bryan, I don't know what to say."

"Neither do I." Putting down the beer, he stood. "I wanted you to know about Carol and me, but where do we go from here?"

We? "If you think it would help to talk about it, I'm a pretty good listener. At least I'd like to think I am."

"I'm not interested in talking about Carol today."

Then what? Instead of asking, she watched as he paced to the window and then over to the bookshelf. She'd forgotten how easy walking was for a healthy man, that it was possible to just sit back and let a man do his thing instead of rushing to his side so he could lean against her. Bryan didn't need her, did he? No one did.

Much of the college jock remained in that physically fit six-foot-plus frame, but his worth no longer revolved around his mitt and batting average. He'd taken on a man's responsibilities, and his body had kept pace, becoming even more solid and set than it had been in its youth, competent.

Not just competent. He represents everything you lost—and some things you never had.

He'd crouched and was looking into her box of tapes before what he was doing registered. Heat rose from her chest to her neck and from there to her cheeks. Too late.

Holding up a couple of tapes, he settled onto his knees and faced her. "Yours or Spence's?"

"Mine." She couldn't manage more than a whisper.

"Hmm. I didn't think they were Spence's. Even when we were young bucks going to strip joints and watching porn movies, I knew he wasn't comfortable with that scene."

The heat she couldn't do anything about had spread everywhere. Even her fingers and toes felt hot, and yet she was glad Bryan had found her collection of sex films—and was willing to talk about them. Now if only she could muster the same courage. "He was pretty conservative. Maybe—maybe that's what attracted us to each other. We were both old school, not particularly liberated."

Bryan nodded. Then he put down the two tapes and went back to sorting. She had every right to the stack. Her parents and other relatives were no longer looking over her shoulder and telling her what was and wasn't acceptable behavior for a respectable girl. Just the same, their lessons and lectures remained, fighting with her body's primitive needs.

He held up one. *"Ripe and Raw,"* he read. "I've seen that one."

"You—you have?"

"Yes." He rocked back on his heels. "Does that surprise you? Lara, when things go bad in a marriage, sex is often one of the casualties. At least it was for me."

"Me too," she blurted. "I mean—oh, you know how sick Spence was. Our—our sex life wasn't very important."

"The title *Ripe and Raw* didn't work for me," he said. "With the vampire element, I would have chosen a title that reflected that."

Warning herself not to wimp out, she took a deep breath. It was time to let the deeply buried Lara into the sunlight. "But it was more than vampires. It was also about a woman learning to embrace her sexuality." *Which is what makes it one of my favorites. My fantasy.*

"True."

Dropping the tapes, he stood and walked over to where she was sitting. She couldn't remember the last time she'd been this close to him or any man other than her husband. Nerves jumping, she ordered herself to stay put. But damn it, how many times had she dreamed about her skin touching a man's? Breathing in his scent? Feeling his touch? And Bryan wasn't just any male body, he was her friend. Separated. On the way to being like her, single.

"What?" she asked, unnerved by his heat sliding over her.

"You're a beautiful woman, Lara. We dated a few times before you and Spence became serious and Carol and I— Why didn't you and I connect?"

Because you scared me. Every time I looked at you, I saw male animal, primitive, sexy. "Who knows?" *Stop being such a coward!* "Maybe because you stuck me with the dinner tab that time."

"Ouch. I'd forgotten that. Wait, you'd offered."

"Only because you were about to lose your mind waiting for your scholarship to come through."

"So you took pity on me?"

Never. "There were some good times back then, weren't there? All of us ready to take on the world. Untested and stupid."

"Stupid? Wait a minute, I think I take exception to that. Do you ever want to go back to those days?" He sat on her chair arm, his elbow brushing her shoulder. Once again her nerves zinged.

"What? No, I have no interest in living life over again."

"You sound as if your life is behind you. It isn't."

How had he gotten so wise? She might have asked if she could have concentrated on anything except his body and the way hers was reacting to it. Two days after Spence's death, she and his sister, who'd been staying with her, had come home from making funeral arrangements. Janet had poured herself a glass of wine and gone outside to read the paper and watch the sunset. On the brink of joining Janet, she'd taken her wine into the bedroom and closed the door. Then, not once questioning what she was doing, she'd stripped off her clothes, taken her vibrator out of the nightstand drawer, lain down on the just-changed sheets and touched the vibrator to her clit.

The moment the toy's energy hit her, she'd arched and clamped her teeth to keep from crying out. She'd never climaxed so fast or felt so out of control. And when she could think again, she'd curled onto her side with her hands between her legs and cried because she'd been so damn needy.

Would she rocket off into another climax if Bryan touched her the way she had? Beyond caution, she leaned against him and drank of his strong heat. "I'm not saying the good years are behind me. In fact, I'm thinking about going back to school."

Was his breathing deeper and more rapid than it had been before she pressed her arm against his? "You are? You already have a degree."

"In business administration. I hate business administration."

His rolling laugh made her smile. She might have concentrated on it more if her awareness of him wasn't so high. "I always wondered about your choice."

"You did?"

"Yeah." Taking her shoulders in his competent hands, he positioned her so she could look up at him without having to turn her head. "You got such a kick out of life, things like those marathon bike rides and cross-country skiing we nearly killed ourselves doing. I just couldn't see you stuck behind a desk."

Bryan worked for the telephone company. She wasn't sure what he did, some kind of engineering, but he was outside more than indoors as evidenced by his wind- and sun-hardened skin. "I wish you'd told me that back then. That way I wouldn't have screwed up my career choice. Thanks a lot, *buddy*."

"Why did you take the route you did?"

"You would ask that. I wanted job security. Growing up with a father who changed jobs the way a lot of men change their clothes, having an in-demand career within what I perceived as a stable industry was important to me."

"It isn't anymore?"

"No. Life's so short. If I don't grab it now, when will I?"

"Good. Good."

About to ask him to explain further, she stopped and simply looked at this man who'd been part of her world for many years. No matter how many things they'd done together, how many shared experiences, she'd always kept a certain distance between them and now suspected he'd done the same thing. They were friends, spouses of other people, not intimate.

Today she needed intimate. Needed sex.

Feeling braver and more reckless than maybe she had in her entire life, she reached up and stroked his chin. Stubble burned her fingertips, the sensation seeming to spread throughout her. Startled, she dropped her hand.

"I want to be a teacher. To be surrounded by children, to go crazy from the noise and energy, to feed off that energy and enthusiasm for knowledge."

"To feel alive again." He covered her hand with his and brought it back up, resting it against his cheek. The contrast between his hard jawbone and warm flesh was almost more than she could handle.

"Yes. I want to feel alive again."

TWO

*H*E DIDN'T RESPOND, didn't so much as move a muscle. But his chest was moving, and wasn't that a vein pumping at the side of his neck? Awareness of those nuances, to say nothing of their closeness, was like a jolt of electricity. Standing, she took a step as if to put distance between them, but she'd been alone for so long and needed to touch. To feel.

To fuck.

Turning around, she stood with her hands balled at her sides, heart going like a spent racehorse, belly knotted and hot. Danger! The kind of danger that comes with standing at the edge of a cliff with the wind pushing against her back.

More than danger. Promise.

Calling herself insane and needy, she retraced, stopping only when her knees pressed against his. She couldn't think of a single word to say and didn't want him to speak.

Pick me up and throw me on the floor. Rip off my clothes, force my legs apart, bite my breasts and fill my mouth with your tongue. Shove into me like we're animals in heat, make me scream. Fuck me the way they do on my tapes, the way I've never experienced.

The silence went on, breathing its own breaths, raging through her until she thought she might fly apart. Then, because the alternative was lonely hell and a night with an unfeeling vibrator, she took his head in her hands and kissed him.

Don't ask why I'm doing this, please.

He didn't. Quite the contrary. He spread his hands over her waist as if she needed steadying. At first she couldn't do anything except accustom herself to the nearly forgotten sensation of her lips touching a man's. Exposing herself this way made her feel so damn vulnerable, and part of her tried to pretend that it wasn't happening. But even if he rejected her, at least she'd have tried and would survive the attempt.

Reason faded. In its place sensation sparked to life. This was no peck between friends. No risk taken between strangers. She was a lonely woman and he a lonely man, alone in a house that no longer meant anything to her, heat flowing through her veins.

Without breaking the contact, he slid off the chair arm and into the seat, bringing her with him. She sat on his lap with her legs pressed against his and his cock hardening, his arms on her back, crying without tears, lips against lips, breathing together.

Unnerved by the flood of emotion, she nearly convinced herself she didn't want this heat, this energy. But she did! She couldn't live without it.

Not at all sure what she was doing, she opened her mouth and slid her tongue through the space she'd created. Finding his

unbelievably soft inner lips, she closed her eyes and took herself
to a place without chairs and walls, without her too-skinny ass
nestled on his lap.

In this new space there was only a breeze's soft hum and fireflies walking across her skin. Energy.

He must have floated into it with her and understood its
colors because his hands were sliding up and down her arms as if
following the fireflies' lead. Weightless, she turned her flesh over
to him, her mouth sending a message that spoke of acceptance
and need and hunger.

The breeze continued its soft song, but now something was
being added, a deepening to the hunger, a sensation close to
pain in her womb. How new and untested she was as a woman,
almost like a reborn virgin.

Sudden fear pounded into her. What if he rejected her because, despite her marriage license and the wedding ring she no
longer wore, she knew pathetically little about fucking?

*Back off. Tell him that kissing him was a mistake and you won't let it hap-
pen again and he should leave as soon as you find the title to the truck.*

But if she did, she might not survive the night.

Would hate her cowardice.

Confused but knowing how important this scary thing they
were doing was, she drew back. His features remained blurred.

"I'm sorry," he muttered. "I shouldn't—"

She pressed her forefinger over his lips. "I started this."

"Why?" he asked around her finger.

"I, ah, chalk it up to too much time alone."

"It's more than that."

"How do you know! I mean, what makes you think that?"

He'd kept his hands on her since the kiss began. Now he ran them down her hips, the journey intimate and maddeningly slow, pressure reaching deep into her and increasing her awareness of her cunt. How would she react if he touched her there? Could she keep from begging?

"My job often takes me near electricity," he said, his fingers walking over the front of her thighs. Her breath whistled. "I can sense when a line is live just by getting close to it. There's a humming, a kind of invisible spark, a warning for lack of a better word. All those things are happening to you."

"Are my feet on the floor? If I'm grounded, then you should be safe, shouldn't you?"

He smiled but didn't otherwise acknowledge her attempt to lighten the moment. Maybe she'd leaned back a little more because his features had come into focus, and yet was she looking at a face she'd ever seen before? What was it about seeing a stranger's face across a crowded room and the absolute certainty that her world had changed as a result? She might never have experienced that particular romantic jolt but she'd dreamed.

This wasn't a dream.

"I don't know what I'm supposed to say," she admitted.

"Nothing. For once in your life, go with instinct."

"For once?"

Shaking his head, he dropped his gaze to her lap. Following his lead, she noted how close his fingers were to her crotch. He pressed. "What are you thinking?"

Rip off my clothes. Place your head between my legs and drink. Slide a finger into my ass and another in my pussy. Flip me onto my back, lift my hips, take me doggy-style.

"I-I'm not sure I am."

"Do you want me to stop? Are you about to slap me or yell 'assault'?"

"No." *Oh God, do you have any idea how good and terrifying being touched like this feels!* "I, ah, I trust you. I know you wouldn't do anything I didn't want."

"What *do* you want, Lara?"

For you to take over. Play the masterful male. Be caveman and throw me over your shoulder and haul me off to where you can have your way with me.

Have your way? Did anyone say that anymore?

"Do you know what your body is saying?" His tone was lower than it had been a moment ago.

If a body spoke through its cunt then yes, she heard the message loud and clear. Even with her shorts pressing against her core and trapping too much sensation, moisture was finding its way to the surface. Maybe his fingertips had found the wet heat.

"Yes," she whispered. "I do. It's getting turned on."

Laughing, he hugged her to his chest. She might have stayed within his arms' shelter if he hadn't helped her sit upright again. All traces of his laughter were gone, and his new expression fascinated her. This man was her friend, buyer of unneeded pickups, acceptor of her erotic video collection.

Start one of those videos, the one with spanking in it. Position me facedown on your lap, stroke my cunt while you slap my ass. Don't let me up. Spread my legs and strike me there, let me struggle and howl.

A wave of reckless courage she'd never thought herself capable of grabbed hold. Throwing off the mantle of her upbringing and maybe everything she'd ever believed she was, she slid off his lap and onto her knees. Resting her forearms on his knees, she looked not into his eyes but at his crotch.

"I'm not the only one who's turned on." A little more courage and she'd close her mouth around the mound, jeans and all.

"What do you want to do about it?"

Spence had never asked anything remotely like that. Sex happened under the sheets with the lights off and her nightgown pushed up around her waist.

"I want to sle—I want to have sex with you."

His jaw actually dropped. A heartbeat later, he recovered enough to close his mouth.

"What?" she asked as her courage dripped away. "I said something I shouldn't have?"

"No, no." He ran his knuckles over the side of her neck, nearly making her levitate. "I just didn't think the words would come that quickly for you."

Was there a world beyond this room? Were there people who thought of things other than how much they needed sex? Who fucked when and where they wanted and didn't carry a lifetime's worth of baggage around? "Maybe I should back up. Return to familiar territory. Be the woman you think I am."

He ran his hands into her hair, fingertips brushing against her temple and sending a chill down her spine. "Let me tell you something, Lara. I never truly understood the woman you presented to the world. I sure as hell didn't know her."

She started to speak, but he shook his head. "The conservative dress, conservative conversation, keep-me-at-arm's-length attitude. I respected it, but I always wondered if I was seeing the real you. And if that was all there was to you, I felt sorry for you."

"Sorry?"

Tipping her head upward, he touched his lips to the tip of her nose and then her forehead. Current raced through her, biting and heating. "What I said about my being able to sense electricity? That kind of thing sometimes happens between men and women, messages being given out. Hell, maybe it's all instinct and not something we have control over. But today's the first time I've sensed it in you."

"I'm, ah, glad."

"So am I. I'd wonder why you were locked up like that, whether . . . I don't know, whether there was something physically wrong in the sex department."

Instead of being shocked, appalled or angry, calmness settled over her. Knowing she was doing the absolutely right thing, she slid her hands along the insides of his thighs. Holding his breath, he spread his legs.

Throw him across the bed, take scissors to his clothes, tie him spread-eagle to the posts, climb up next to him, close your hand and then your mouth around his cock. Run your teeth along his length and watch him struggle, hear him.

"Maybe there was something off-kilter, but today's different."

"You want?"

"I want."

Smiling his beautiful smile, he unbuttoned the top button on the practical old shirt she wore to do yard work. With that simple gesture, she ceased to think of herself as a gardener and embraced what it meant to have breasts and a pussy. Her fingers found his cock. She kept them there, the touch so light she wondered how much he could feel through the layers.

Giving her no hint, he concentrated on the rest of the buttons. He spent a great deal of time on the task, watching her the whole time. Yes, she occasionally twitched and couldn't help wondering how her small breasts compared to Carol's, but mostly she simply placed herself under his safekeeping. Her body might be crying out to be fucked, but this afternoon was too precious for everything to be played out in a matter of moments.

Rake your nails over his chest and leave your mark on him. Take his nub between your teeth and watch his expression. Pull on it with your hands on your breasts, rubbing, rubbing.

There. The last button no longer doing its assigned task. Because she hadn't bothered to tuck it in, he only had to pull it up to finish the job. Her thighs felt the strain of being on her knees for so long, but she resisted lowering herself because she wanted to remain as close to him as possible.

Can you read my thoughts? Do you have any idea what I'm thinking?

Still watching her through now half-closed lids, he pulled the blouse off her shoulders. The soft, limp fabric slid down her sensitized arms. She could have waited for him to make the next move, but for once she was going to be an equal partner, if not the aggressor. Shrugging out of it, she tossed it as far as she could.

"Lean against me," he said.

So much for initiating. Eager for anything and everything, she rested her waist against his bulge and slid her arms between his buttocks and the chair. Pulling her even closer, he reached behind her and unfastened her bra. The no longer wanted or needed armor relaxed. She would have finished that bit of disrobing if he'd given her the chance, but he obviously wanted to be the one to pull the straps down her arms.

Then he pushed her back, still holding on to the straps. Leaning away as much as she could without losing her balance, she silently gave notice that she wanted this too. Smiling a little, he complied. The bra landed on top of her blouse.

Naked from the waist up. On her knees before a man. Alive. Oh God, alive!

Standing before him with her arms and legs spread, cuffs holding her ready for him. Watching him approach, seeing the vibrator caught in his fingers. Shivering and struggling and nearly dying as he placed it in her and turned it on.

When he cupped and lifted her breasts, she studied them in a way she never had. They were no longer simply standard-issue body parts, because Bryan was handling them as if they were her gift to him.

"Beautiful."

Hiding behind silence, she placed her hands over his and stroked his knuckles as he massaged and caressed. How strange it felt to participate in her own arousal, how strange and wonderful!

He suddenly released her breasts, but before she could think to voice a protest, he took hold of her waist and brought her close again. When his head descended, she arched her back, offering up her breasts. Capturing one, he sucked it into his damp and warm mouth. A river of heat raced through her to fill her cunt with need. Whimpering like some wild creature, she pushed into him.

The vibrator dancing in her, held in place by his hand flattened against her labia, head thrashing, fingers and toes curling, fire lashing her cunt and belly. Screaming and begging, then whimpering when he cranked the invasion up all the way.

He sucked, then pushed her out with his tongue so he could close his teeth around her nipple with his lips providing a protective cushion. Drawing back, he brought her breast with him while she remained in place, increasing the pressure. A voice she'd never heard told her to lean into him now, which created a whole new sensation, an even greater surrender. Fascinated by the play and what it was doing to her overloaded cunt, she took her breast with both hands and pulled it free.

Immediately, she offered the other to him, and while he brought it under his control, she wiped saliva off the free nipple and put her fingers in her mouth.

How strange for him not to be questioning what she was doing. Strange and incredibly wonderful!

But no matter how much she loved this, her back and knees and thighs couldn't indefinitely keep up so she again freed herself. Settling onto a hip with her legs tucked under her, she tapped the carpet next to her.

"Invitation?" he asked.

"With a provision. First, off with your shirt."

Nodding as if they'd just come to a logical decision about a logical situation, he stood and pulled his shirt over his head. He wore no undershirt, unlike Spence, who'd always . . .

No Spence! Let him go.

"Shoes?"

"Of course."

"You too."

Laughing because what the hell did shoes matter now that she'd thrown her bra in the discard pile, she unfastened her sandals and shoved them away. He looked just a little ridiculous holding on to the chair and leaning over so he could untie his tennis shoes, and that endeared him to her. He kicked off one shoe then held out his foot so she could deal with the sock. Taking pity on him, she tended to the other shoe and then the sock. Then, not allowing herself time to question and critique, she brought that foot to her mouth and kissed his big toe.

"Are you sure? That's not the best smelling—"

"Do you mind?"

"Hell no."

"Then shut up and experience."

He was right. The aroma was hardly spring flowers, but lordy, did she love the feel and mostly the contours of a healthy man's foot. While he balanced himself with the chair's help, she sucked and kissed and sucked some more. His toes were surprisingly long, all except for the littlest, which looked like an afterthought and barely had any nail.

"What happened to it?"

"Stepped on by a horse when I was five." His eyes were on her breasts. Because she was leaning over, they hung from her rib cage. *They're part of me. Take me, take them.*

Take me? Oh, hell yes!

Drawing his foot free, he sank to his knees. Then he almost roughly pushed her back until she was sprawled on the carpet with her legs hung up under her. He let her straighten them, then his arms bracketed her and he lowered himself so they were chest to breast.

Bathe my breasts with your tongue. Wrap ropes around them, put on nipple clamps, paint them red or black, tattoo them. Claim them. Make them yours.

On the verge of tears again, she wrapped her arms about his neck and brought her mouth to his. She understood closed-mouth kisses, civilized expressions of love and affection. But civilized had no place here. How could it when she'd give anything to have her raw fantasies come true?

Confused by the multitude of emotions, she handed him kisses that were both shy and bold, unsure and wildly determined. Fire licked her breasts and belly. If she had a knife or scissors, she would have shredded her shorts.

Why the hell hadn't she taken them off?

Because they're all that stands between you and rutting like some animal in heat.

But she was in heat, deep down hungry, bone marrow inflamed, pussy crying and screaming and nearly coming just from thinking about Bryan's swollen cock jammed deep inside her.

She tried to sit up. "I can't—I can't . . ."

He stopped her. "You can't what?"

Had she spoken? "I'm so damn desperate."

"Shh, shh," he muttered and again lowered her to the carpet. One hand rested over her collarbone while the other gently stroked her cheek. "It's all right, Lara. Everything you think and feel and do is all right."

"It . . . is?"

"Don't you know that?"

She didn't know anything, especially not the woman who was clawing her way out of the cage she'd spent her life in. The one imagining bondage and rough sex. That creature was so complex, and right now she wanted everything to be simple, skin against skin, two bodies becoming one.

"I'm going to take off your shorts," he told her in a tone a father might use to get a child to do his homework. "And then your underwear. And then I'll do the same, and we'll take it from there."

Thank you for knowing all the things I don't.

That wasn't true, was it? she amended while he worked with the snap at her waist. She'd made love, even had sex. What she hadn't done was fuck.

Wrapped around him like an octopus, arms and legs tight against his body, fucking standing up with his hands gripping her buttocks to keep her in place, pummeling him as he pummeled her, nipping his chin, yelping when his nails dug into her, leaning back and driving into him, throwing back her head and screaming.

She lifted her buttocks off the ground but otherwise lay there like some damn rag doll while he dispensed with her shorts. Her panties were lavender and nearly covered her navel, and she'd bought them not long after the doctors had told them that they'd be wise to settle Spence's affairs. On days when she'd barely had time for a shower, she'd put these or the yellow pair on because the colors were bright and new.

Now they were a gift to the man she was about to fuck.

"You don't have a stomach," he said, his fingers light on her pelvis. "I want to see you eat."

"Not now."

"No, not now." Lowering his head, he lightly ran his lips over her nonexistent stomach.

She shuddered. Her cheeks were on fire and between her legs, oh God, between her legs— "I thought . . . I thought you were going to, ah, strip."

"Soon, my dear, soon. Doing sex right takes time."

"It does?" By the time she'd gotten the words out, he'd buried the tip of his tongue in her navel. Whimpering, she grabbed his hair and held him in place.

She was swimming somewhere, floating in some invisible place peopled by just the two of them. His tongue-touch was so damn light, like butterflies touching down over and over again.

Deep in sensation, she sank into herself until she found her core. This was no longer simply where, maybe, a new life might one day begin, mysterious folds of soft, sensitive skin, the seat of her greatest frustration and sometimes brief and never fully satisfying relief. At this moment, her pussy, her cunt, existed for one reason. To receive and express pleasure.

"Thank you, thank you," she chanted

Although her fingers threatened to cramp, she couldn't concentrate enough to relax her grip. He must have understood how lost she was in herself because everything he did was about her. Those incredible lips of his claimed her throat, breasts, even the unbelievably sensitive skin on the insides of her upper arms. Mewling, she ground her hips against the carpet. Then, bending her knees, she planted her feet and lifted her pelvis as an unspoken gift to him.

His fingers closed over her wrists. When the pressure continued, she turned what little ability she had to concentrate to the job of releasing his hair. He rewarded her by bathing her nipples with his mouth.

"Something different now," he whispered. "But first, do you trust me?"

"Yes. Yes!"

"You believe I would never hurt you and that I know what I'm doing?"

"Yes."

"Good. First, I no longer want these." Standing, he uncere-moniously removed his jeans. At the sight of his bulging briefs, her mouth dried, and she silently thanked him for not expecting her to participate in his disrobing. Her arms felt like cooked spa-ghetti, and she could barely manage to swallow.

"Ready for the next step?"

"Yes." Speaking nearly strangled her. "Yes."

"My cock is pretty much standard-issue." His fingers were looped around the elastic on his briefs but still, waiting. "Noth-ing outstanding. Average size. I've been circumcised."

"Do it! Please!"

Head tilted a little as if determined to read her every expres-sion, he held out the elastic and pushed down. When the mate-rial hung up on his cock, he took hold of the still-hidden organ and lifted it out.

Now his cock stood proud and hard and dark and insistent against his paler body. *Beautiful. Oh yes, beautiful.* Sudden moisture flooded her mouth. Was she really wondering what it would feel like in there?

Yes!

Her eyes started to burn, compelling her to blink. "So . . . strong."

"It hasn't had much use lately."

"I'm sorry."

"I'd rather put up with frustration than lie and pressure in an attempt to exercise my husbandly rights."

It shouldn't be like that. You deserve a loving woman's willing body.

If only she had the courage to tell him that, to ask him what sexual frustration felt like for a man and share her own experiences, to let him into her secret world, but that wasn't going to happen today. Tomorrow, maybe. Hung up on the possibilities, she studied his gift. "Not—not standard-issue. Bryan, it's so big."

"And your conclusion is based on extended observation?"

"You know it isn't."

"Sorry. I shouldn't have said that."

Because you know what a damn stupid novice I am in what everyone else takes for granted? "It's all right."

"No, it isn't," he said and stepped out of the garment they had no use for. "I hate people who build themselves up by making less of others. You are who you are, Lara. A faithful wife."

"I'm a widow."

Dropping to his knees beside her, he brought his mouth to within a few inches of hers. "Not today. Today you're a desirable woman, and I'm a lucky man."

Desirable? Had she ever been told that?

Before she could dig through her memory for the answer, he pressed his lips against hers, and it didn't matter. He kissed her long. Hard. Pressure filled with challenge and promise. She answered with all her strength.

In the home team's dugout, the benches filled with leather mitts and hard plastic protective cups but no players, the stands empty as well. Bryan sitting straddle-legged on hard wood while she crouched before him, mouth around his cock, taking him deeply. Thinking home run.

"Now, close your eyes and relax."

Had they been open? And how could she possibly relax? But

she'd told him that he was worthy of her trust and wanted that to be a deep truth.

Keeping his hands on her, he moved from her side to between her legs. She widened her stance. Cool air rolled over her all-but-dripping pussy. Could he smell her? Did he have a problem with that? Spence had—

No! Not Spence!

Sliding his hands under her buttocks, he lifted her. Eyes still resolutely closed, she helped brace herself. Were they going to fuck right now? About to ask him to slow down, she instead whimpered as his expelled breath feathered over her labia. A moment later, she dug her nails into the thick carpet fibers, head thrashing. Instead of trying to protect herself from further assault, she trembled and waited, her pussy offered up as his gift.

Another moist breath, this one even warmer and more forceful, pushed a sob from between her lips.

"Like it?"

"Oh my—oh, yes."

"I'm just getting started."

Sex now. Fucking and being fucked now?

No! Oh God, no!

Her body reacted violently, shaking and shuddering at the same time and her pussy muscles clamping. Only when she'd started the downhill slide did she realize that he'd touched his tongue to her sex.

Her stomach roiled. She wasn't sure but thought she might have broken a nail.

"Again," he muttered.

Not just a quick, light touch this time but stronger and longer, sweeping forward, gliding over hot and swollen and so-sensitive flesh.

"Oh shit!"

"Like it?"

"Oh shit, yes!"

"Then hold still."

What? What did he think she was capable— "Shit, shit!" she all but screamed as he worked past her electrified folds to the source of more fluid than she'd known she was capable of. "Oh, fuck!"

Yes, a nail definitely broken as witnessed by the sharp pain when she tried to claw the carpet. It didn't matter.

His tongue everywhere. Circling her opening, dipping in and then stopping, holding there awhile, retreating.

"Shit!"

"You're cursing."

"I-I can't help it!"

"Do you want me to stop?"

"No, no!" Digging her heels into the fibers, she arched as high and vulnerably as she could.

Instead of heeding her too-obvious demand, he forced her to wait. At least he gave her something to think about by again forcefully expelling his lungs against her cunt. She lost touch with and interest in her house, the day, tomorrow and yesterday. There was just this furious craving deep inside and the core-deep knowledge that only he could satisfy it.

"Please," she whimpered, her legs trembling.

THREE

WHEN THE SECONDS STRETCHED OUT, she opened her eyes and fought to focus. He was on his knees but stretched out with his upper body nearly on the floor and supported by his elbows. His hands were under her, his fingers extended to her waist. Strange that she hadn't felt his hands go there but, then, maybe her pussy's responses overpowered everything else. Settling back down, she waited out the hot sparks in her thigh and calf muscles then wiped sweat from her throat.

"What—what am I supposed to do?"

"You really have never done this? Cunnilingus, I mean, oral sex?"

"No."

"Damn him."

"Don't. I never asked—"

"Don't explain. What went on in your marriage is none of my business."

"It wasn't just my marriage, Bryan. I've told you about the one-horse town I grew up in, and you've met my parents. You know how conservative they are."

"You could say that."

"Sex . . . ah . . . the only thing my mother ever told me was what products to buy when I started menstruating and that nice girls never let boys touch their breasts or *down there*." Even with the hunger between her legs, she laughed. Nearly cried. "I didn't until I got married."

His expression sobered. "Today is almost like being with a virgin."

She didn't want to be a virgin! She wanted to be fucked! And to fuck. "Then pop my damn cherry."

That made him laugh but she caught a serious undertone to the sound. A new expression spread over his features as he slid his hands out from under her and straightened, no part of his body touching hers. She closed her legs until they found his knees. "What is it?"

"We can't fuck. Ah, shit!"

"What? Bryan, I can't—"

"I want to. Believe me, I want to." Grabbing his cock, he squeezed it as if fighting with himself. "Are you on the Pill?"

Comprehension dawning, she shook her head. "I stopped when . . . when I knew there wasn't going to be any more sex. I was having side effects and . . . "

"Are there any condoms in the house?"

"No. What about you? You're—"

"I never cheated on Carol."

Before today. Looking up at Bryan, with her pussy still exposed and accessible, she realized she'd never had a more open conversation with a man. She could hide behind the virgin label and wait for him to make the necessary decisions, but damn it, she'd played that game throughout her marriage and didn't ever want to again.

She and Spence hadn't once talked honestly about what they wanted from sex let alone tried anything except the missionary position, and she deeply regretted that two sexual conservatives couldn't have at least tried.

"I'm not surprised you didn't cheat. You never struck me as a man who'd stray."

"Just because you didn't receive any signals doesn't mean they weren't there."

"Signals?"

His hold on his cock seemed to tighten. "I sent you a number of signals when we were dating and after we stopped, but you acted oblivious. Were you?"

Good question. Vital question. "You made me nervous. I was always aware of you, but I didn't know what to do with what I was experiencing."

"You do now."

"Yes." His jaw set, he shifted as if getting ready to stand. *No!* "Bryan, look, ah, my period is about to start." She ran her fingers over her breasts. "They always get sensitive just before. I'm not ovulating."

"You're sure?"

"I'm not going to get pregnant."

"That's not the only— Look, I swear, you don't have to worry about anything I might give you."

So this is what honesty feels like. "Neither do you."

"I never thought—"

"If I was any other woman, you would have wondered about other sex partners, wouldn't you?"

"Probably."

For some reason that made her laugh, the sound bringing with it a new sense of freedom. "So, now that we've covered the subject, where were we?"

"Interruption over?"

"I should hope the hell so."

"If that's the lady's wish—"

"It is."

"Then I'm ready to go back to eating you."

Closing her eyes, she flattened one hand over her belly while the other went to a breast. She was already caressing herself when he lifted and positioned her legs over his shoulders. His hair brushing an inner thigh was all it took to rekindle her fever. This time she concentrated on technique and response, mostly response. He began at the lowest point of her entrance and slowly worked his way up. Ah, yes, her outer lips, his tongue gliding over them but leaving the even more sensitive inner flesh alone.

Damn, damn! Her videos showed sexually liberated people doing exactly this. Once, wondering if she'd ever experience that, she'd punched a wall.

Now, now!

"Oh God." Her grip on her breast tightened and became almost painful. "Oh God."

Bryan lifted his head. Before the loss of his tongue and lips registered, he slid his fingers over her sopping opening. One finger—at least she thought it was just one—dipped in and stayed there.

"Oh shit!"

"Swearing again."

"Feels good. So damn good."

"Yeah. It does."

The instant he again replaced his hand with his mouth, her eyes closed. She existed where he touched and nowhere else. She was aware of the tightness in her breasts and an all-encompassing heat, but her arms and legs didn't interest her. This incredible man's lips were pressed against her flesh. She'd thought she'd be embarrassed to have a man lap her sex juices and smell her ripe arousal, but those concerns didn't matter to the bitch she was becoming.

A bitch? Oh yes, bring it on!

"Ah—so good. It—oh, yes."

He again lifted his head and repositioned himself so he was on his knees with his buttocks resting on his heels. Just nervous enough for the emotion to add to everything she was feeling, she willed her muscles to remain limp while he pulled her closer until her ass was on his thighs and her legs on either side of him.

"What are you doing?"

"No questions, woman. Just experience. And trust."

Ah, yes, his finger back inside her, pushing ever deeper, with other fingers and both palms trapping her cunt beneath them. When he began a simulated fuck, it was all she could do to breathe, to find a flicker of strength.

Everything was about her pussy, her cunt, her clit. She existed as a receptacle for Bryan's knowledgeable hand.

Heat. More and more heat. Body melting.

No, not melting. Climbing. Reaching. Twitching.

"Ah—ah!"

"What?"

How could she respond when that powerful finger had been joined by another and the pace—the mind-bending pace of his thrusts had doubled in speed?

Climbing even faster. A wild horse charging up a hill, head high, with the wind streaming through its mane.

"I'm—oh shit! I'm coming."

The climax slammed into her, a hot, hard, long blow that arched her spine and pressed her legs hard against his sides. Yes, she knew this sensation because she'd gone in solitary search of it countless times. But always before, she'd turned off the vibrator afterward so she could lie there, panting and unnerved but safe.

But he wasn't stopping! In and out, in and out he powered. Lightly slapping a breast, the inside of her thighs, her belly.

"Ah! Ha!"

"Ride it! Ride it!"

Explosion followed by another by another, muscles knotted and screaming.

"Stop! Oh, shit, stop!"

Something winked and went dark. When the light came back on, she sensed she'd briefly lost consciousness. Her mouth gaped, her muscles shuddered, arms limp at her sides and her body awash in her own sweat and sex juice. "Holy shit."

"Like it, did you?"

Open your eyes, blink away the red haze and focus on him.

"Did you like it?"

"I never . . . holy shit."

"You never what?"

His fingers were still housed in her, but thank God, he'd put an end to the bone-rattling manipulations that had hurtled her over the edge. *For the moment.*

"I had no idea a climax could be that intense."

"It went on a long time, right?"

After resting a moment, she managed a rueful smile. "You'll have to ask someone who was keeping track of time. I'm out of breath. Bryan? Thank you. Thank you so much."

"You're entirely welcome." He slowly withdrew his fingers and held up his hand so she could see the juices soaking it. Her pussy felt oddly hollow as if it might remain stretched and open forever. She couldn't imagine being able to survive having anything in it, not even his cock.

His cock.

About to ask what he wanted her to do so he could experience the same release, she watched as he brought his glistening fingers to her mouth. When he touched her lips, she licked herself off him. What a bold and wonderful thing to be doing!

"I didn't know you'd climax so quickly. I wanted—hell, I wanted to bring you along slow and draw out the pleasure."

"There wasn't a slow gear in me," she admitted, not at all embarrassed at having acted like some animal in heat. *Animal? So that's what all the excitement's about, what I've been fanatisizing about.*

Sharp pain replaced her lassitude when he backed away and brought her legs together. Damn, but the cramp in her calf hurt! She started to sit up so she could massage it, but he pushed her back down and kneaded the knotted muscle.

"Better?"

"Much better. Bryan . . . "

"What? Don't climb back into your cave now."

He was right. Too much had opened up for her to want to backtrack after the giant step she'd just taken, with his help. "You—you still have a hard-on."

"I can't argue that."

"I want to do something about that."

"Hmm. What did you have in mind?"

She'd never been asked the question. Although Spence had always had to work for a long time before he climaxed, she'd mutely accepted his pace while she provided the willing but eventually tiring receptacle for his laboring cock. Fortunately though, thanks to her video collection and imagination, she had some ideas.

One in particular.

"Sit down." The new woman she'd become at the moment of her first no-holds-barred climax pointed at the love seat.

Although he gave her a puzzled look, he did as she ordered. Watching his retreating buttocks made her long to clamp her hands around them and squeeze. Then once she had him where she wanted him, she'd reach between his legs and take hold of his balls and give them a decidedly friendly squeeze.

How bold you're becoming.

He perched more than sat on the edge of the love seat with his hand cradling his swollen penis. If she didn't take charge right here and now, the poor man would have to take matters into his own hands in more ways than one.

The uninhibited creature who'd taken over her body crawled to him. Grabbing his knees, she forced his legs apart, although *force* wasn't really the operative word since he was more than willing to comply.

"I've never done this before," she admitted. "I've seen it done—on videos—but if I do something wrong—"

"If you don't want—"

"I want! You have no idea how much." *And need. Mostly need.*

And yet when she opened her mouth around the potent-looking head, part of her screamed at her to turn tail and run. She could do this another time, later, after they'd gotten to know each other better and had had sex in conventional ways.

Conventional and modest and boring defined your marriage. You don't want anything more to do with that.

Bowing to the greater wisdom and truth, she closed her lips around a man's cock for the first time in her life. How big it was! Dense and more solid than she'd expected, wonderfully warm with those engorged veins pressing against the roof of her mouth. Tasting of sweat and something else. Precum. His body's signal that he was ready.

The women in her movie collection expertly took more and more cock into their mouths until the tips pressed against the backs of their throats, but she might gag.

Go at your own pace. Make it good for both of you.

Ah yes, that was doable. Easy. wonderful.

Her saliva already coated every microinch of the sleek surface, prompting her to close her lips as best she could to keep him from sliding out. There was no way she could have anticipated what housing his most precious possession would feel like. How strange to be both in charge and submissive, to control and be controlled!

The contrast between heavy blood-swollen strength and satin-like skin fascinated her. Using her tongue and the roof of her mouth and the insides of her cheeks, she explored and then explored some more.

Her pussy, which should have been all but dead and buried following its violent exercise, sighed back to life. Bryan was leaning away from her with his neck and shoulders resting against the love seat back, hands gripping the armrests, legs splayed and ass barely on the seat. He'd rolled his head to the side and was watching her with an expression she couldn't possibly call relaxed.

Eager. Anticipating. A bit anxious.

No need. I might be a novice in giving head but I'd never hurt you.

After rewetting the insides of her lips, she let her mouth glide up and back along his length. She kept pressure going but varied it, perhaps guided by impulses in her mind, or ruled by her own body's growing fever.

In and out. In and out. Turning her head to the side and repeating. Moistening her lips again. Jaw aching slightly, tongue forced out of the way, heat flowing between them. Nodding. Shaking.

Deeper. Deeper. Good, now a little more. Ah, feel his tension. Smell his sweat. And yours.

When he gripped her hair, she knew the gesture had nothing to do with making her stop. Going by his harsh breathing, she knew he was reaching the edge of his own cliff. She'd brought him near the point of climax—she!

Her own electric heat sparked higher, taking her deep inside herself. Although she continued to work him, she could no longer concentrate on what her so-called technique was doing to him—not with her clit insisting and wetness dribbling down the inside of her right leg.

Rocking back on her heels, she slowly freed him. The instant the head popped out, she slid her hand along his damp underside. Grateful for her short nails, she lightly fingered his balls.

"Shit," he hissed. "Fuck."

"I agree."

"What?"

"Never mind. I'll show you."

Standing shouldn't be that hard, but her muscles had been replaced by heat-softened rubber. By widening her stance and keeping her arms out from her sides, she managed the complex position. Still, she didn't trust her ability to do this for more than a few seconds.

But she needed those seconds, needed to look down at his splayed and vulnerable body, acknowledge the fiery gaze.

She'd told him she was in charge, but all she'd ever been a party to was the damn missionary position and she'd be damned if she'd resort to that! Those videos, the X-rated instructional manuals, what had she learned from them?

He was on a love seat with his weight on his spine, his lap empty, his cock like a living gift. Embracing the new Lara, she climbed onto the seat facing him, her legs outside his. Taking his cock again, she pressed it against her belly. *Ah, so strong, his skin there even softer than hers.*

Gripping her tight around the waist, he arched up, teeth exposed. Laughing, she leaned away before he could reach her breasts. Relaxed in the wake of their playful moment, she increased her hold on his cock and then lifted herself slightly, taking the trapped organ with her.

"What are you doing?" he demanded.

"Seeing how much I can stretch you."

"The hell you are!"

With that, he started tickling her. "No! Damn it, no!" she squealed but didn't try to get away. Damn it, concentrating was— "Stop it!" Desperate for relief, she pinched his nostrils shut. All that earned her was some openmouthed breathing on his part and increased tickling.

"No fair!"

"Like what you're doing is?"

"All right, all right!" Although concentrating was nearly impossible, she let go of both his cock and nose. To her great relief, he ended his attack. Still, she didn't trust him.

"Truce?" he asked.

"Hmm. Maybe."

"What do you mean, maybe?"

"I'm thinking. Give me a minute." Even as she spoke, she lifted herself as high as she could. Taking hold of his cock again, she slid it between her legs and eased down, slow and satisfying and filling her hole. "There." *Oh God, yes!*

"There what?"

Gritting her teeth, she gave him a mock glare. "I found a place to park the source of this little disagreement."

He wiggled his ass. "I like being parked there."

So did she, in spades. How glorious being filled by him felt! She was complete now, a newly wrapped package, her pussy doing what it had been designed for.

When she planted her hands on his chest for balance and rocked forward, his cock pressed against her forward wall; leaning back changed the sensation. After letting her explore for a short while, he pressed up on her rib cage. The instant she lifted her weight off his pelvis, he slid forward so his knees were fully bent and his lower legs were at a right angle to his thighs, allowing him to use the floor for leverage. Even so, his movements were limited.

If there was going to be any honest-to-goodness friction, she'd have to provide it. Fine, wonderful, about damn time.

"I'm going to ride you, cowboy." Still bracing herself on his chest and shoulders, she started working her body up and down, up and down.

"People don't ride cowboys."

"Don't correct me! Just shut up and enjoy."

"I intend to."

Concentrate! Dig deep inside for strength and energy.

Obeying was simple and absolutely vital. Repeatedly pistoning herself, she studied her breasts' furious bouncing. Her mouth hung open. Despite her sopping pussy, the internal friction kept building, heat burning, temperature rising. Her vision blurred. She no longer existed except to fuck and be fucked.

Up. Down. Cunt muscles clamping around the hard power buried so deep, she thought she felt him clear up to her navel. Up, down. Up again, sucking in air. "Ah! Ah!"

"Ride me! Damn it, ride me!"

A fire between her legs, sweat streaming between her breasts, his hand suddenly at her throat and pushing her back, letting go of his chest with one hand and reaching behind her, clamping her fingers around his thigh to keep him from knocking her off.

"Ride me! That's it, ride me!"

"Shit, shit!"

The erotic pressure on her throat ended. Gasping, she concentrated on his hands back around her waist. Although she trusted him in a way that went all the way to her core, she shifted her hand from his chest to the love seat back. Able to maintain a more upright position now, she sent fresh messages to her straining thighs. Up. Down. Faster, faster. Again, again, yet again. "Oh God, damn, I can't . . . can't do this much . . . much longer!"

"Turn around."

"What?"

"Turn around."

All right. Okay, fine. With his help, she lifted herself off him and stood on melted-butter legs as her suddenly empty cunt begged and demanded. Needing to be filled again as she'd never wanted anything, she turned around and lowered herself over his groin. Her thighs easily held her above him while they worked together to position his cock at her entrance.

Down again, her inner tissues gloriously swelling. Skewered. Oh yes, skewered by this man's cock.

Claiming her waist again, he drew her back toward him. Reaching behind her, she used the back as her brace. Her legs were widely splayed, arms and legs taking much of her weight.

Now he did most of the work. He repeatedly powered up and into her, his cock not as deeply buried as it had been before but the head pressing against her forward wall. A sensation akin to powerful static electricity shot through her.

"Okay!" she hissed. "Oh shit, okay!"

Another thrust, more static.

"What?" she demanded. "Oh shit, what!"

"Found it, did I?"

"Found . . . what?"

"Your G-spot."

How did she know? But the electrical charges or whatever they were had sent her someplace she'd never been before. Had bit and clawed and stung. "Fuck, oh shit, fuck! Oh my God!"

Explosions, fast and furious, the house burning down! "Coming! Coming!"

More, more, too much! His cock adding endless fuel to the fire, G-spot exploding and her muscles wrecked.

Terrified, she threw herself forward. There. Better. Slightly better. The explosions no longer the end of the world but now a hot and wonderful swift-running river.

"Yes, yes, yes!"

As her climax subsided, she knew one thing and one thing only. He was ejaculating into her, grunting and gasping.

"I CAN'T MOVE."

"No one said you had to."

They were lying on the carpet with throw pillows supporting their heads, on their sides, arms draped over bodies. His hair was a bird's nest, and she kept having to push her own hair out of her mouth with her tongue. She wasn't sure but she thought he'd been the one to suggest they do their recovering as close to the love seat as possible. She knew she'd gone after the throw pillows. As for whether either or both of them had fallen asleep, who cared?

The only thing in the whole wide world that mattered was that she finally and completely understood the meaning of the word *fuck*.

"Thank you," she whispered, then leaned forward and kissed him.

"Thank you yourself." He winked.

"I'm serious." Tears were heating her eyes, but she didn't think she was going to cry. "What happened between us— I am so unbelievably grateful."

"I'm glad I could accommodate." His expression turned serious. "I don't mean to make light of our having sex. I didn't know it was going to happen any more than I believe you did, but it was what both of us needed."

Me maybe more than you. "I feel as if I've been reborn." After kissing him again, she propped herself up on her elbow and regarded him. If she'd ever been more relaxed or content, she couldn't remember. "At some point, I felt the old me slip away. It might have been at the umpteenth *hell* or *damn* or *fuck,* all words I don't think I've ever spoken."

"You haven't?"

"No. A nice girl doesn't, you know. Only, you did in that *nice* girl today. Buried her. I kept having these hot fantasies. Full bodied as if they'd been around for a long time."

"I can't change you, Lara. What you did and said and experienced and thought has always been in there waiting to come out."

"Waiting for you to bring her out."

She supposed he could have pointed out that any red-blooded male could have provided her with her first earthshaking climax, but thank goodness he didn't.

"What are you thinking?" Rolling onto his back, he pulled her down on top of him.

Grinding her belly against him, she lifted her head so she could meet his gaze. "The question is, what are you thinking of?"

Laughing, he clamped his hands over her ass cheeks and held her in place. "Not so fast. I'm an old and tired man who needs some recuperation time. Besides, I believe I promised to buy dinner."

"Yes, you did." Easy laughter rolled out of her. "I hope you brought a lot of money because I'm starving."

"Me too."

So get up. Draw straws to see who takes the first shower. Offer to go Dutch treat. Instead, she ran her tongue over the base of his throat. "When we're done eating, I hope you'll come back here with me."

"For tonight?"

Eyes open and honest, she pulled in air that smelled of sweat and sex. "More than tonight, much more."

Still smiling, he patted her ass. "Damn, but I like the new Lara."

"I fuckin' love her."

STUD MUFFIN WANTED

LENA MATTHEWS

ONE

ARON FELT LIKE CRYING. According to the latest quiz in *Blaze Magazine*, she was a Little Miss Goody Two-shoes. Someone who obeyed the law, saved herself for marriage and the woman men would most likely take home to meet their mother. But for a successful businesswoman, it wasn't the way she wanted to think of herself.

The questions blared at her like Hester's scarlet A. Staring at the quiz, Karon tried to recalculate the figures, attempting to blur the lines of her answers in hopes that maybe she could somehow come out a little better—or dirtier—as the case might be. Karon didn't necessarily want to score a Brazen Badass rating—she just wanted to score higher than a thirteen-year-old Catholic schoolgirl.

It was depressing and embarrassing, in that order. Karon had known for a while that her love life could use some spicing up, but she didn't realize just how bad it had become. Karon had spent much of her youth studying and working hard, never making time for partying or having a good time. After graduation she had been too busy getting her business off the ground to worry about something as trivial as orgasms.

Karon was extremely proud of all her accomplishments. At thirty-four she owned her own business, and she'd recently purchased a beautiful house near the beach. Yet she was letting a stupid magazine make her feel like shit because she'd never played naked Twister.

Scowling, Karon dropped the magazine on the seat next to her, facedown. It was bad enough that she felt like crap from reading the article, she didn't need to see the picture of an emaciated twenty-year-old girl, who'd been airbrushed to perfection, staring back at her while she wolfed down a plate of pasta that would kick her carb limit off the Richter scale. Being a plus-size woman in a Twiggy world was hell on a person's ego.

"Hey, girl, sorry I'm late," breezed her best friend Jacque Bois as she slid into the booth opposite Karon. "You will not believe . . . What's wrong?"

"Nothing." Karon didn't want to get into it with Jacque. There was no way the beautiful, willowy, never-had-a-bad-date socialite would understand.

"Don't tell me 'nothing.' You look like you're going to cry. Did you lose a sale?"

Karon shook her head. At this stage in her career, the loss of a client, while disappointing, wouldn't send her into tears. As the broker of her own real estate company, Karon was quite successful and led a comfortable life. That's why it was so disappointing that her personal life was such a disaster. What personal life? According to the quiz, she didn't have one.

"No, it's just—" Karon stopped short of explaining. Closing her eyes, Karon reached for the magazine and plopped it down in front of Jacque, pages up. It was better to just get it over with.

"How naughty are you?" Jacque looked up at her with confusion etched on her pretty brown face. "What? Did you find out you're a big ol' whore?"

"Just the polar opposite." Karon grabbed the magazine and turned the page over, pointing at her ranking. "I'm a Goody Two-shoes."

A slow smile stretched Jacque's lips as she read the description. "Ahh, sweetie, what's wrong with that?"

"'What's wrong with that?'" Karon gasped. *Was she mad?* "What do you mean 'what's wrong with that'? I'm thirty-four years old. Who wants to be considered a Goody Two-shoes at thirty-four?"

"Umm, a nun?"

"I'm not a nun." Karon's loud voice turned several curious faces their way. "I'm an attractive woman, in my prime, and I've never had anal sex."

Jacque looked around them with wide eyes. "Could you please calm the fuck down before you get us kicked out?"

"How can I be calm about this? I graduated from Berkeley for Christ's sake, how the hell is it possible that I've never played Spin the Bottle?"

"You haven't?"

"No." Karon shook her head as she snatched the magazine from Jacque's hands. "Listen to this. Have you ever made out with a stranger? No. Have you ever been skinny-dipping? No. Have you ever had oral sex? No."

"Hold up." Jacque raised her hand to silence Karon. "What do you mean you've never had oral sex?"

Karon sighed. She so didn't want to go into this with Jacque, who had a standing grudge against Karon's on-again, off-again beau. "Walter doesn't like it."

"He doesn't like it?" The disbelief on Jacque's face would have been amusing if it wasn't for the subject matter at hand.

"No. He doesn't think it's . . . very hygienic, if I recall correctly."

"Hygienic?"

"Would you stop repeating everything I say?"

"I'm sorry, but, girl, I'm in shock. I've never known a man to turn down head."

"Well, now you do."

"But you liked it when he did it to you, right?"

"If he didn't think it was hygienic to do it on him, how do you think he felt about doing it on me?"

"Shut . . . up." The words were said slowly, as if Jacque couldn't comprehend Karon's words.

"Jacque!"

"I'm sorry, but damn. Not hygienic? Talk about selfish."

"It's not a big deal."

"The hell it isn't."

"You're not making me feel better." In fact, she felt eons worse. Karon just wanted to crawl under the table and die.

"Sorry. What about college? You had to have done some of these things in college."

"You think? Let's find out." Karon opened it up again and read aloud. "Engaged in bondage? No. Had sex in the bathtub or water? No."

Jacque raised a brow as she asked sarcastically, "Not hygienic enough for Walter?"

Karon sent Jacque a searing look before continuing. "Gotten or given a rim job. Eck! No. Videotaped yourself having sex? No. Watched someone masturbating? No. Engaged in a threesome? No." Karon plopped the magazine back down with a resounding thump. "How sad is that? I'm sure threesomes had to have been somewhere on my college curriculum but I skipped it because I had to take advanced courses. I had absolutely no fun in college, you know why? Because I tried too hard to get ahead. My freaking college roommate was a one-handed lesbian and she had more action than me, and you know what? That never bothered me, until now."

Jacque bit her lip, fighting back a smile as she pointed to a question Karon had skipped over. "How about this one? Have you ever had a same sex experience?"

"I said my roommate was a lesbian, not me."

"Just checking, Boo."

"I'm depressed and you're amused." She would probably be amused too, if they were having a conversation about someone else.

Jacque shook her head quickly, as if to clear her mind, before reaching over to pat Karon's hand. "Okay, I'm sorry. But, Karon, why do you care what this trashy magazine says? It's destructive literature in its highest form. I mean really, who writes this shit anyway? 'Your Orgasms and You.' My orgasms and me are just fine, thank you very much. I don't read this crap for a reason. Neither should you. You're an intelligent, beautiful woman. Why are you even giving this a second thought?"

"Because it's sad."

"Okay, here's what we're going to do." Jacque pulled her briefcase up onto the table and took out a pen and a notepad. "We're going to make a list of everything you want to do and you're going to do it."

"Yeah, right. I can just see me calling Walter up and saying, will you come over and masturbate for me?"

"First, eeww." Jacque shuddered at the image. "Second, you're not going to do this with Walter. You've spent enough time with him as it is. Five years was five years too long."

"Yeah, then who?" Walter may not be perfect, but he was the only man in her life right now. Neither one of them wanted to be tied down so their dating situation, even though it looked odd to outsiders, had really worked for them. But Jacque was right, that relationship was over for good.

"You're going to go out there and find some young, hot stud and indulge in carnal acts until you walk bowlegged for days."

"Where am I supposed to pick up this young, virile man? High school?"

"No, we're going to go on a manhunt. For once, you are going to let all your inhibitions out and do everything on the list. Consider it an early birthday present to yourself."

"Orgasms, the gift that keeps on giving."

"Now you're thinking." Jacque waggled her brows jokingly. "Okay, first go over this and check how many you've already done."

That was going to be easy, thought Karon as she took the pen out of Jacque's hand. A college science-lab partner, a former business associate and Walter didn't amount to much when it came to the quiz. Quickly going down the fifty-question list, Karon meticulously crossed out five items before handing Jacque back the pen, with a "now what" look on her face.

Jacque quickly counted the checks and looked up at Karon with a look akin to horror across her face. "Five?"

"Five," Karon repeated stoically. If Jacque thought Karon's problem could easily be fixed, she had another think coming.

Their waiter came to the table, interrupting their silent stare. "Are you ladies ready to order?"

"Give us a bottle of Cabernet and two of the largest plates of fettuccine Alfredo you have," answered Jacque, without even looking at the menu.

"Yes, ma'am."

"Hey, I'm calorie counting, remember?" Another bane to her almost perfect existence was her never-shrinking pants size. She could put up a brave front for the rest of the world, but the fact that she hadn't been a single digit since birth never left her mind. It wasn't a plus-size-friendly world, no matter how successful she became. Even Oprah lost weight eventually. "Honey, we can't plan your sexual revolution on an empty stomach."

"And a hot plate of garlic bread," Karon said to the waiter, who looked as if he were visiting the *Twilight Zone*. If they were going to screw up her daily intake, they might as well do it in style. "Make it fast."

"Yes, ma'am."

"See, that's what you need." Jacque gestured toward the disappearing waiter. "A man who'll obey your orders and not ask questions."

"If he's limber, that would be great," quipped Karon sarcastically.

"This is a serious matter. Now, how many of these do you really want to do?"

"You can cross number thirty-seven off to start with."

Glancing at the number in question, Jacque swiped her pen across it, marking it out. "Okay, no foot worshiping. How about this one: would you have sex in a public restroom?"

Karon scrunched up her nose as she thought. The idea of having sex in a bathroom seemed sexy in a way but the practicality of it made her nauseated. Public bathrooms smelled and were littered with germs.

"I take it the idea doesn't appeal to you."

"Not really, but put it down with a question mark next to it."

"Okay," Jacque agreed as she went over the list. They ended up compiling a list of twenty-seven things she definitely wanted to do, thirteen things she might do and five things Karon wouldn't do at gunpoint. "I think we've got some good stuff here."

Taking a sip of her wine, Karon shook her head in amusement. It had been fun making the list, but she'd never work up the nerve to actually approach a stranger to do it. "You're as crazy as that list."

"What? Oh come on, you have to do it."

"I'm not going to put an ad in the paper and say, 'Stud muffin wanted. Horny, limber men with no inhibitions need only apply'."

"Hmm . . . " Jacque had a calculating look in her eyes as she tapped the pen on the notepad.

"I'm kidding, Jacque."

"But it's not a bad idea."

"No." Karon felt desperate, not crazy.

Rolling her eyes, Jacque sighed. "Fine, we'll go out to a club."

"Yes, because that's so much better. Have you heard of sexually transmitted diseases?"

"Have you heard of condoms?"

"Nothing is a hundred percent protective."

"And you wonder how come you scored so low, Miss Goody Two-shoes." Jacque crossed her arms over her chest. "Let's just go out tonight and look around for possible candidates. If you don't see anyone who floats your boat, groovy, we'll try a different avenue, but you have to try. I mean, really, what do you have to lose?"

A million things came to mind such as her dignity and respect, which she quickly pointed out to an amused Jacque.

"Yes, and what great bed partners they make."

This is what I get for arguing with a lawyer, Karon reminded herself. Besides, Karon had gone her entire life being good. It was time she did something for herself.

"Fuck it, I'm in," she said, to Jacque's delight. *What would it hurt to try?* Besides, Karon would turn thirty-five in the not too distant future and there was no way on God's green earth she was going to reach that milestone without having tasted semen.

TRISTAN DODSON NEEDED MOUTH-TO-MOUTH resuscitation. He never would have thought the word *masturbation* would have a life-altering effect on him, but here he was gasping for air because a ravioli noodle went down the wrong pipe. Things wouldn't have been so dramatic if he hadn't been eavesdropping in the first place, but when the words *anal sex* came floating over the fake plants sitting on top of his booth, he couldn't help but listen.

And listen he did, because not only did he figure out that

the speaker was in dire need of an orgasm, he also figured out who the speaker was. There was no way he could mistake the husky drawl of Karon Bower anywhere. The voluptuous Southern beauty had charmed him from the first moment he had met her at a small-business association meeting and he'd been trying to ease his way into her path ever since.

The casual friendship they'd maintained over the last few years had only whet his appetite for her, but now it seemed as if fate was going to sugarcoat the how and why—he just had to concentrate on the when.

A concerned waiter hovered over him with a pitcher in his hand. "Would you like some more water?"

Taking in a deep breath, Tristan waved him away. "I'll be fine." Just as soon as he swallowed his lungs back down anyway. His eyes burned with unshed tears, but pain aside, Tristan had never felt so good. Karon was on a manhunt and Tristan planned to do everything he could to make sure he was lined up in her shot.

The voices on the other side of the booth had lowered, but he'd heard enough. Gesturing to the waiter, Tristan paid his bill, refusing to have his killer meal boxed up. He had a plan. As he stood, he overheard her companion say she was running to the restroom and decided to wait until the woman passed him before approaching Karon.

Gazing at Karon as her companion passed by, Tristan took a moment to drink in the lovely image she emanated. As usual, she wore a fashionable two-piece suit that catered to her plush figure, showing off her luscious curves to his avid eyes. The soft cream color complemented her smooth, pale skin and dark auburn hair, making Karon look like a succulent peach, ripe for the picking. And Tristan was a sucker for peaches.

Tristan had always been attracted to Karon, but the right situation had never presented itself for him to try to take things further. Now knowing that the classy, lush lady in front of him wanted someone to fill her backside somehow made her more approachable.

Go figure.

"Karon," Tristan called her name, causing her to jump and accidentally knock her wineglass over. Fumbling like a Three Stooges impersonator, Karon grabbed at everything around her, trying to stop the impending mess.

"Good Lord, Tristan." Smiling, she wiped at the puddle on the table, moving her notes discreetly to the side, as if he needed the paper to understand her wants. Her words had been branded in his memory, ensuring him an afternoon of unappeased desire. "You startled me."

She was startled! Hell, she should try coughing up ravioli out her nose. "I assure you, it wasn't my intention."

"I didn't see you come in." Her smile was as inviting as her warm personality and one of the many things he liked about her.

"I've been here for a while."

The light seemed to dim a bit from her big blue eyes as she glanced around the restaurant as if trying to garner where he had been sitting. "Did you enjoy your lunch?"

"Immensely." He nodded. "Although it tasted much better going down than it did coming back up."

"What?"

"Nothing." Tristan watched her for a moment wondering

what move to make. He thought about saying "Are you enjoying that tossed salad, and by the way, I'm willing to toss yours" but decided against it. Something about Karon didn't scream anal licking on the first date. "So how is everything in your world?"

"Great." She beamed, obviously lying through her teeth. A woman with a great life wouldn't be crying in her pasta. "Work is great. Life is great. Everything's . . . great."

"May I sit down?"

"Of course." Nervously, she moved her plate over, trying to cover her notes, but spilling her sauce on the tabletop in the process. "Goodness, I'm a complete mess today."

"Let me help." Leaning over, Tristan grabbed her notes from under her plate, wiping the white sauce off with a napkin. This was not how he had intended the plan to go, but he was quick on his feet and more than willing to let opportunity in when it knocked.

Squeaking, Karon reached her hand out to grab the papers, but instantly froze when Tristan turned them over and began to scan. Unable to believe the extent of the list, Tristan paused in reading it to look back down at Karon in shock.

What he saw surprised him even more than the conversation he had overheard. It didn't make sense that an attractive woman of Karon's caliber and style could have made it this long without doing some of the things on the list. They lived in the twenty-first century for Christ's sake. Who didn't give head these days?

Sitting down across from her, Tristan sat the sheet down in front of him, mindful to keep his hand on it. "This is quite a list you have, Karon."

"It's not mine," she denied quickly, reaching across the table for it.

Picking the paper up quickly, Tristan turned it around until it faced her. "You mean the list that says 'Karon's sexual to-do list' doesn't belong to you?"

"It belongs to my friend."

Tristan tried to bite back his smile, but it truly was a losing battle. "Your friend named Karon?"

"It's a very common name." Her lies were getting weaker by the moment and he could tell she knew it. Karon's face flashed from embarrassed to sheepish. Heat rose, bringing her skin color close to that of her glorious hair. She looked adorable as hell.

"Yes, I suppose it is."

Hand held out, Karon wiggled her fingers toward him. "Can I have it back please?"

"Sure." Tristan didn't need the list anymore. The words were practically burnt into his memory. "But do me a favor."

Letting out a relief sigh, Karon folded the paper and slid it under the table. "What?"

Tristan reached into his pocket and pulled out his business card. Quickly scribbling his home number on the back, he handed Karon the card, much to her confusion. "What's this?"

"This is my number. Office and cell on front, home on the back. I want you to call me before you head to the bar looking for your"—pausing to remember the exact phrase he'd overheard, Tristan cocked his head to the side, watching Karon's jaw drop open in surprise—"stud muffin. I'm more than willing to help you fulfill your wish list."

"Oh my Gawd. Oh my Gawd." Her eyes were as wide open

as her mouth and her rosy complexion seemed to become ashen.

Tristan knew being amused was wrong, but he couldn't help himself. "Call me, Karon." Sliding out of the booth, Tristan bumped right into her companion, who looked between the two of them inquisitively. "Karon, I presume?" he enquired teasingly.

"Huh?"

The confusion on her face was priceless. "Exactly."

TRISTAN COULDN'T CONCENTRATE for the rest of the day. His eyes continuously wandered to the phone, as if willing Karon to call. When his secretary did tell him he had a call, he jumped on the phone, only to be disappointed that it wasn't his blue-eyed beauty.

The thought that Karon might not call him never entered his mind until two hours had passed and she didn't. Tristan didn't think he was God's gift to women or anything close to it, but there had been something there between the two of them. He had always thought so anyway.

When he had first met Karon she had been in a relationship, so gentleman that he was, Tristan backed off. Maybe that was his first mistake. He wasn't one to poach on another man's territory, but now in hindsight, it seemed as if this Walter fellow wasn't handling his business.

What kind of man didn't like head, giving or receiving?

His cock began to stir behind the steel confines of his zipper at the image of Karon—pretty, voluptuous Karon—pleasuring him with her mouth. A sliver of pleasure rippled down his skin at the thought of her down on her knees before him. Her full breasts displayed wantonly as she stroked her hand up and down his shaft, her plump pink lips—

A loud buzz startled Tristan, who sat up quickly in his chair, knocking his knee into his desk. "*Fuck!*"

"Call on line one, sir."

Stars shot behind his eyes, his arousal quickly faded, making way for the pain now coursing through his joint. Gripping his knee, Tristan muttered every obscenity known to man under his breath.

"Sir." His secretary buzzed the intercom again, her nasal voice ringing loudly over the speaker. "Line one."

"I got it!" he damn near shouted, vowing to himself to change the volume on his phone at the next opportunity. "Yes."

There was a brief pause, before a hesitant drawl whispered across the line. "Uhh . . . Tristan?"

Eyes widening in recognition, Tristan released his knee and gripped the phone tighter. "Karon." Calming his breathing, Tristan waited a few beats, hoping she would say something. After an uncomfortable length of silence, Tristan spoke again. "Are you going to speak?"

A soft chuckle floated across the line. "I'm trying to figure out what to say."

"It shouldn't be this hard to talk to me, Karon. We've known each other for a while."

"We are, at best, casual acquaintances."

"Not from lack of desire on my part, I assure you."

Karon paused again, causing Tristan to wonder what she was thinking. The phone wasn't the way he wanted to do this. Tristan wanted to be face-to-face with Karon so he could read her expressions and see her smile. Hell, he would be content to see her frown, as long as he was able to see her.

With a deep breath, Karon blurted out the speech Tristan was sure she had worked on for the last two hours. "I want to explain to you what happened at lunch. I don't want you to get the wrong idea about what you saw."

And heard. "I think I have the right idea, and I think you know I do."

"It's not what it seemed."

Her denial made him grin. "You mean you're not frustrated with your sex life?"

Karon's gasp was answer enough. "I . . . I . . . "

"There isn't a need to feel embarrassed." The last thing Tristan wanted was for Karon to be embarrassed. Aroused, orgasmic, his, yes—embarrassed, no.

"Says you."

"How about dinner?"

"I don't think that's a good idea."

"But I do." Tristan leaned back in his chair, mindful of his tender knee. "We can talk about your list some more."

"You're deriving far too much pleasure from the idea that the list could be mine."

Smiling, Tristan couldn't believe Karon planned to continue denying the list. "Come on, Karon, we both know that it's yours."

"No, *we* both don't know that."

"Okay, I know and you're confused. But either way, it's nothing to be embarrassed about."

"I'm not embarrassed," she denied heatedly.

"Then prove it. Meet me tonight."

"I'm not going to discuss this in public."

Even better. "Then how about my house?"

"How about your house what?" Suspicion clouded her voice, amusing him all the more.

"How about you come over and we discuss your list . . . excuse me, *the* list in more detail."

"You're killing me, Tristan." Her smooth voice wrapped around him like a silk blanket as her suspicion gave way to wary amusement. "It was just a joke. A little joke between my friend and me."

"Then let me in on the joke. Tonight," he insisted, not willing to let Karon ease her way from him now. "Do you have a pen to take down my address?"

"You're just not going to let this go, are you?"

As if he could. "Not in this lifetime."

"Drinks then—but only drinks," Karon warned after she took down his address.

"I'm easy."

"That's what I'm afraid of." Karon hung up before he could comment. Not that Tristan could think of a damn thing to say to save his life. She was coming over. The hard part was over.

TWO

*Y*OU KNOW, SOME might consider this blackmail," Karon stated as soon as Tristan opened the door. Why mess around with pleasantries when she could get right to the point? It wasn't as if she had many secrets left from him now anyway.

Laughing, Tristan stepped back, gesturing for her to enter his home. "You're looking lovely as usual, Karon."

Karon tried to steel her heart against him. She refused to let Tristan charm his way out of this. The man was lethal and he damn well knew it. Charm, looks, money, he had it all in spades, but Karon refused to be bowled over so easily. "Can the compliments, Tristan. All I want to hear from you is muttered echoes of pain as I pummel you to death with my Fendi bag."

Grasping his chest comically, Tristan teased, "Death by couture, my mother would approve."

"Spawns don't have mothers." Squinting up at him, Karon thought back to the speech she'd rehearsed over and over again on the drive to his house. There was no sense in denying the list any longer. It hadn't worked at lunch or over the phone so she sincerely doubted it would work now, especially with him looking as good as sin on Sunday.

There should be a law against a man being that attractive. Dressed casually in khaki pants and a white shirt that complemented his tanned skin, Tristan looked fit to man a yacht on the lake, not to have drinks over blackmail. There always seemed to be an air of confidence around him. He charmed without being overly charming, and he easily impressed without being a show-off. So why he felt the need to resort to blackmailing her—of all people—Karon hadn't a clue. But she was only going to give him five minutes, then she was out of there, blackmail or no blackmail. There was only so much beauty a woman could take in one sitting.

"Are you interested in coming all the way in or just plotting my demise in the entryway?"

"Full of jokes. You know, if the situation had been reversed and I were in your place, I would be far nicer."

"Oh I plan to be nice, Karon." Tristan winked at her slowly as heat began to blossom in her cheeks. "Very nice."

Karon didn't know if that was a threat or a promise, but either way, it sounded pretty damn good to her. Torn between amusement and exasperation, she followed Tristan down the hall to his living room, admiring his taste on the way. His home was as immaculate and beautiful as she had expected, with warm tones painted on the walls and plush furniture filling the large room. The real estate agent in her admired his home and roughly sized up the place in her mind, total worth and value.

"I'm not selling my home, Karon." Tristan spoke as he watched her face, amusement laced throughout his voice.

Damn. Karon hid her smile with cool disinterest. "I'm just admiring—"

"Sizing," he insisted with a smile.

"Admiring," Karon continued, refusing to let him know he was right, "your lovely home."

"You know, you're adorable when you lie. It was one of the first things I thought this afternoon."

Abruptly turning around, Karon faced him with what she hoped appeared to be a bored look. She refused to make this into a big deal. It had taken her a few hours to get over her embarrassment, but even she could see the humor in the situation. The worst part was that she was the one who had put herself in this predicament in the first place. *Damn magazine quizzes.* "The gloves come off and the bell dings."

"I don't know what you're talking about."

"Now who's the cute liar?"

"Think I'm cute, do you?" The corner of his mouth quirked up in amusement as Karon raised a brow mockingly.

Really, who was he trying to kid? "Don't even start with me. You know you're cute. So stop the seductive act. I know why I'm here."

"I thought you were here to talk about your friend's list."

"Do you want me to hurt you?"

"In the right circumstances, I might."

Bemused, Karon shook her head. "You weren't spanked enough as a child."

"Care to make up for it now?"

"Tristan!"

"Karon!" Laughing, Tristan walked away, heading toward the

bar in the corner of the room. "You're too innocent for your own good."

"Yes, and that's the problem, remember," she agreed, watching the way his butt moved under his slacks as he walked. Tristan had a nice-looking ass. Biting down on her lip softly, Karon wondered what it would feel like between her hands. Startled at her train of thought, Karon turned away from him and sat down quickly on the golden settee.

When did Jacque take over my brain? This wasn't like Karon at all. She didn't write sex lists, complain about her love life or stare at men's rumps. Her grandmother Aggie would die if she could read the thoughts going on inside Karon's head. Karon hadn't been raised this way . . . but then again, it was why at thirty-four she felt unsatisfied with her sex life. It was hard to be a lady when all she wanted to do was act like a wanton woman.

"So you're going to admit the list is yours now?"

"I admit nothing." Gathering her reserved cool, she looked up at Tristan, who was back at her side with a tumbler in his hand.

"Bourbon right?"

Surprised, Karon looked up at him in awe. "I can't believe you remembered that."

She could count on one hand the number of times they'd had drinks socially, and yet he hadn't forgotten. The fact that he'd locked away in his memory bank something so unimportant about her had Karon's mind whirling. Either he was more interested than she had given him credit for or he was one hell of a player.

"I make a habit of remembering beautiful ladies' drinks of choice. It makes it much easier to seduce them later."

"Is that what you plan to do, Tristan? Seduce me?"

"Do you want me to?" he questioned, just as brazen as he pleased. Moving to the sofa to her left, Tristan watched her intently, waiting for her to reply.

Karon didn't answer his question, mainly because she couldn't think of an easy answer. She had good self-esteem, honestly she did, but the very idea that Tristan's overall goal was to get her into bed with him just didn't compute. He could have his choice of women, and men for that matter, why was he really wasting his time on her? "Why did you ask me over?"

That was the question she wanted an answer to the most. She had her own fantasies for that answer, lots of fantasies that mainly consisted of her straddling him and riding her list to the finish line, but she wanted to hear what he had to say. Just so she didn't embarrass him or herself.

"Several reasons."

Not good enough. "Like?"

"Like I didn't like the way you looked when I left."

"You mean my faint resemblance to a woman about to die from a heart attack?"

"Exactly." He smiled.

"The wide-eyed, scared rabbit look doesn't work for you, huh?"

"Not from you it doesn't." His look and tone implied much more than he was saying. It sounded more like a sensual promise than a mere comment.

Karon didn't know what to make of Tristan's new persona. He was sexy, hell she'd always thought that, but now it seemed as if there was more heat behind his umpf, and it was directed toward her. *Her,* for goodness sake. Someone must have spiked her Slim-Fast, because Karon was surely imagining things.

If it weren't for her giant faux pas at lunch or her control-top panty hose, she'd be all over him. But now, Karon didn't know for sure if he pitied her or wanted her. It was bad enough she had been caught with the list, but to be caught by someone she knew and admired horrified her. "Oh, why did you have to come over to our table?"

"Because I heard how sad you were."

Startled, Karon sat as if frozen, staring at Tristan in shock. *Heard. Dear Lord, let that be a Yankee euphuism for something else, like . . . hell in a basket, nothing was coming to mind.*

"What do you mean 'heard'?" *Please, please, please let me be wrong.*

Tristan's cheeks bloomed with heat, confirming Karon's worst fears before he even opened his mouth. "I guess I didn't mention yet that I overheard your conversation."

Damn it all to hell and back. "But how?"

Clearing his throat, Tristan had the grace to look a bit sheepish. "I was sitting at the booth behind you."

"Behind me," Karon practically screeched, more embarrassed now than she had thought possible. "So you just didn't run into us and see the list?"

"No, I heard the list, or the beginning of the list first."

Flinching involuntary, Karon wished that her bones would melt and she could slip through the fibers of his carpet. Not only did he see her list, Tristan had heard what they were saying. "And you still came over?"

"As if I could have stopped myself after hearing what I did."

"What exactly did you hear?"

"Enough."

Enough didn't answer her question. Karon needed to know how mortified she needed to be. "What exactly is enough, Tristan?"

Setting his glass down on the coffee table, Tristan rose and moved across the room to stop in front of his fireplace. Gone was the amused man who had first let her in—in his place was a serious one. Tristan looked almost as uncomfortable as Karon felt, and it made her feel better, if only for a second.

"Tristan, tell me."

"I know that your boyfriend—"

"Ex-boyfriend."

"Sorry, ex-boyfriend Walter, who I might like to add looked like a stuffed prig the day I met him at the Christmas party, isn't a very . . . giving lover."

"You heard that?" Karon closed her eyes in horror, unable to comprehend how her luck could be so bad.

"And more," he added softly.

"More!" *Take me now, Lord. Just take me now.*

"I didn't want to tell you that part."

"Of course you didn't. It's hard to seduce a woman who's dying of embarrassment."

"First," he stated firmly, walking back to her side. "You have absolutely nothing to be embarrassed about. And second, I hadn't planned on seducing you."

"You didn't?" Taken aback, Karon completely skipped over the embarrassed thing. Tristan hadn't planned to seduce her. How disappointing.

"No. Seduction has a hint of sneakiness and deception about

it. I'm not about hiding what I want or pretending to be something I'm not."

Good Lord. Tristan's words shot straight to her middle, filling her with a heat she hadn't felt in so long. It was so very obvious what she'd been missing in her love life all these years, if his mere words were turning her insides to jelly.

"I'm serious. I don't want you to be embarrassed with me. There's just no cause."

"I'm sorry, I tend to disagree." Karon stood as well. She needed to move around, to think.

If this didn't count as seduction, Karon was in serious trouble. She wasn't used to feeling like this and it was confusing. She should be mad at him for eavesdropping at the restaurant in the first place, not trying to think of the quickest way to his bedroom. "The way I look at it, I have every reason to be embarrassed."

"That's where you're wrong."

Snorting, Karon faced Tristan with a mocking glare. "You don't think the fact that my boyfriend . . . former boyfriend finds me lacking in bed is something to be ashamed of?"

"The only person lacking was him, Karon. You're a very desirable woman. You're smart, funny and sexy as hell. From what I can tell, there's nothing at all wrong with you."

"You've never been intimate with me," she tossed out before she could help herself and immediately regretted it. *Oh my God. Just stop me from talking. Seal my lips together, cut off my tongue, do anything to shut me up.*

A slow smile spread across his face as he took her hands in his. "Something we can easily rectify."

"I thought you weren't going to seduce me."

"I'm not."

"Then what do you call this?"

"Me."

"Then you're too much for me, Tristan. You heard what I said. You read the list. I'm not prepared for you."

Laughing, Tristan released her hands, allowing Karon to make her much-needed escape to the bar to refill her glass. "You're laughing at me, but I'm being honest. I think we should just pretend none of this ever happened and save me my last shred of dignity."

"That's not going to happen, Karon. I'm not going to back down from this."

Of course he isn't. That would be too easy. "Why?"

"Because I think you're a desirable women who is in the need of some—"

"Therapy."

"No, loving."

"I'm not looking for a lover, Tristan."

"I don't think you need a lover."

"No." Karon was surprised and disappointed in his answer. Part of her had to admit she'd been hoping this was Tristan's way of trying to get her into bed. Not that he would have had to try too hard. "Then what do you think I need?"

"A teacher."

TRISTAN WATCHED KARON as his words sank in. Her smile was hesitant at first, as if she wasn't sure whether or not he was joking.

But in Tristan's mind, there was no need to hesitate. He was dead serious.

There would be nothing more arousing than schooling Karon in the many ways of love. There was nothing she could put on a list or ask him to do that Tristan wouldn't. If it pleased her, it pleased him. To see her eyes dilate with pleasure, to feel her nails press into his back in the heat of passion, was all that he was living for now.

Tristan wanted to drown himself in her essence. To drink from between her thighs until he was sated. Simply put, he wanted Karon and everything she had to offer.

"You think you can teach me?"

"I would love to."

"Better question is, why should I agree?"

"Because it will be better with someone you know, someone who cares that you receive pleasure. Someone who will remember your name in the morning, unlike a mystery man at a club."

"Heard that too, huh?"

Tristan continued. "I'm honest, healthy and you'll always know where you stand with me. I want to experience your pleasure just as much as I want to be the cause of it."

"For someone who doesn't believe in seduction, you're doing a damn fine job of it." With her drink in hand, Karon headed back to the couch, where she sat down weakly.

"I'll take that as a compliment."

"You should."

"Why the hesitation, Karon?" Tristan could tell by her pasty complexion and nervous manner that he had thrown her for a bit of a loop. But now was the time to attack. He knew, really, truly knew, that if he tried to coax Karon, she would bolt behind a wall of civility and they would never achieve the greatness he knew they could.

"I hesitate because I keep thinking of one important thing."

"What's that?"

"If you hadn't overheard me in the restaurant, you would have never approached me now."

So that was what was behind the uncertainty lingering in her pretty eyes. In his haste to make sure Karon turned to no other man, Tristan forgot to reassure her. He would have approached her without the list once he knew Walter was out of her life, but Karon didn't know that. Careful not to crowd her, Tristan sat back down across from her and looked her straight in the eyes.

Tristan didn't want there to be any doubt that what he was about to say to her was true. It was more important to him that Karon believed him than it was for him to put on airs. "It's not sudden interest, Karon. I've always been attracted to you."

Surprise filled her eyes as she studied him. "You've never said anything."

"I'm a bit slow." More than a bit, to both of their detriments.

"Just a tad."

"When I first met you, you seemed to be extremely focused on your career. Your business was just getting off the ground and I, of all people, can understand how romance can take a backseat to your career. So I bided my time. Then I found out you were seeing Walter and I had to wait for the thing with him to run its course."

"You say 'run its course' as if he and I weren't meant to be to-gether."

"You weren't. I knew that as surely as I knew that one day we'd be here. Walter and you never seemed right to me."

"I don't even want to get into that."

"But I think we need to. I think you need to realize that it wasn't you."

"How do you know it wasn't?"

"Because I'm sitting across from you aroused, dying to know what you taste like." Karon's gaze dropped from his face to his groin, forcing his cock to harden further in his pants. Tristan chuckled and sat back farther against the couch, parting his legs a bit so she could get the full visual of his arousal.

Karon quickly averted her gaze, heat blooming in her cheeks. "So—" Clearing her throat, she continued. "If I agree to this, how do we go about it?"

"If?" There were no doubts in his mind that Karon would agree. As aroused as he was, Tristan didn't know if he would be able to let her walk out the door tonight if she didn't.

"Yes, I haven't made up my mind completely yet."

"Liar," he teased. "But I'll let it slide this once. Did you bring your list?"

"*The* list."

Biting back a chuckle, Tristan didn't press the fact. "Sorry, *the* list."

"Yes."

"I say we look it over and decide where to go from there."

Instead of pulling out the list, Karon seemed to edge back farther in her seat. "And you're just going to do them?"

She was still nervous. "No, *we* are going to do them."

Tristan knew if he chuckled as he wanted to, it would definitely ruin it for her. Karon was only a few seconds away from dashing to the door as it was, so he had to go steady and slow. Two speeds he wasn't feeling right now. "Let me see the list."

Karon still didn't budge. "But what if it's something that you're uncomfortable with or if it's something you don't do?"

As far as Tristan was concerned, there wasn't a thing she could possibly ask for that he hadn't imagined time and time again. "Karon, is everything on that list something you want to experience?"

"Yes."

"Then it's something I want to do." Standing up, Tristan walked over and sat down next to her on the couch. Karon maneuvered a bit to the left, giving him more room than he wanted between them. That was never going to do.

Easing back against the sofa, Tristan tried to appear as nonthreatening as possible. He wanted Karon to feel comfortable with him next to her, as she had before this afternoon.

With a deep breath, Karon opened her purse and extracted the list. It was neatly folded in half and when Tristan went to reach for it, she gripped it tighter. "If you make one crack . . . "

Crossing his heart like the good little Boy Scout he never was, Tristan pledged, "On my honor."

"It'll be my fist on your head, not your honor," she grumbled, sitting back and watching him.

Tristan couldn't resist. Leaning forward, he brushed his lips against hers, surprising her and arousing him even more. She was just so damn cute, he couldn't resist. Only his Karon would tell him off while handing him a list of sexual things she wanted him to do to her. What a hell of a woman.

Pulling back slowly, Tristan reluctantly took his mouth away from hers. Her soft lips had burnt an impression in his mind and he couldn't wait to feel them elsewhere on his body.

"Now, back to the list."

Clearing her throat, Karon hoarsely agreed, "Yes, the list."

It was going to take Tristan a while to get back in focus. List be damned, he wanted to make love to Karon now and worry about the consequences later. But this was about her and her needs, not about him and his hunger.

Taking a calming breath, Tristan unfolded the page and choked on his laughter. Karon had numbered and typed the list on her personal stationery. Everything was neat and orderly, just as he'd expect from her.

She had all the positions sectioned together, as well as the places she wanted to make love put together. She even went so far as to rate the different things, from five asterisks down to one, with a little code key at the bottom to explain what they meant. She was anal and adorable and all his.

"What, is something wrong?" Tristan narrowly pulled the list out of her reach as Karon lunged for it.

"No, I was just admiring your . . . orderliness."

"There's nothing wrong with being organized."

"No, there isn't," he agreed with a smile. "I just have a few questions."

"Okay." Folding her hands primly in her lap, Karon sat back and waited patiently, as if in a board meeting.

"Are these listed in the order in which you wish to accomplish them?"

Frowning, Karon moved closer to him to peer at the list. "Is that wrong?"

"No, it's not wrong."

"Are there too many things on the list?"

There wasn't nearly enough. Some of the things were just silly. That really made Tristan want to kick Walter's ass. No woman should have oral sex on her to-do list. It should be a given. "Hardly. The only problem I see is—"

"What?"

"It's not going to take all that long to do this list."

Eyebrows raised, Karon looked back down at the list and then back at him. "It isn't?"

"Well, no. I mean, I would automatically do number one," he said pointing to the five-asterisk-rated cunnilingus, "every time we had sex."

Continuing down the list, Tristan paused at the sexual positions. "And number twenty-one and twenty-two can be done in the same session."

"Really?"

"Sure, we can move from the wall to doggy-style with no hardship at all, after I've gone down on you and you've number two'd me." Pausing, Tristan had to ask. "Have you really never performed oral sex on a man?"

"Would it be on the list if I had?"

"The only things I see that might be a bit more difficult are numbers twenty-six and twenty-seven."

Karon nodded her head in understanding. "Yeah, I didn't think the plane and the train thing would be that easy, but I had to put them on the list."

"We'll work up to it." Tristan assured her with a smile. God, he wanted this woman. "Now for the *might-do* list, is there a particular reason it's not automatically on the *to-do* list?"

"I haven't made up my mind just yet."

Blindfolds, bondage and sex games were definitely on his list. Her *might-do* list was quickly being added to his *must-do* list.

"Now for the rules," Karon interjected, slipping back behind her cool mask.

"Rules?"

"Yes. I want to make sure that this stays friendly."

"Oh, I plan to be very friendly."

Karon clutched her purse closer to herself. "I mean, if for any reason you're unable to perform because of . . . well, because of anything, I just want you to know I'll understand."

She wasn't making any sense. Why on God's green earth would he have a problem perform— *Ohhhh*. "Walter had erectile issues?"

"No, of course not." She flushed, looking away. "I mean, it's more than obvious that I could stand to lose a pound or two."

Tristan never would have thought someone as successful and take-charge as Karon would ever have issues about her weight, especially since he thought she looked perfect just the way she was. "Says who?"

"The surgeon general."

Different strokes for different folks. Tristan was old-school when it came to his women. He liked them built for comfort, not for speed. It wasn't a fat fetish or any other derogatory term. He simply liked women to have breasts he could bury his face in and an ass he could grip as he pounded into them from behind. "Let him worry about his own woman. I happen to like my women shaped like a woman should be."

"And that's how?"

"Just take a look in the mirror, Karon, and you'll be able to answer your own question."

As if unsure how to respond, Karon forged on, ignoring his previous comment. "Another thing that's very important to me is my reputation. Corona isn't a big town and something like this getting out has the potential to damage my good name. I've worked really hard to get where I am. It's a cold, hard truth that men can sleep with anyone and everyone and no one will say a word, but the minute a woman tries that, she's branded a whore and I'm not a whore. Technically, neither are the other women cursed with that label."

Lost in her maze of rambling, it took Tristan a second to get to the heart of what she was saying. Irritation flared through him at the realization of what Karon was insinuating. Startled that she would ever think he might do something so heinous had him seeing red. "I'm not out to ruin you, Karon, just to fuck you. But if we're applying a few rules, I have a few of my own."

Her eyes widened at his cool tone. "Of course."

"First rule, we don't just do a number once. We do it as often as I like. You're not the only one who has some excess energy to burn."

"Okay."

"And secondly, I reserve the right to add to the list at any time."

"There are things you haven't done?"

The awe in her voice calmed him down a bit. There were still so many things that were innocent about her. "There are things that I haven't done with you. Things that will have you acing your next quiz."

Karon seemed intrigued by the notion. "Then it looks like we're both on the same page."

"Finally."

Karon stood as if they were done. "So do you want to make plans to get together, say Friday?"

Tristan stood as well, amused that she thought it was going to end that quickly. "What's wrong with today?"

"Today! You want to get started today?"

"I want to get started right now."

Pulling her to him, Tristan did what he had been dying to do from the moment they first met. He kissed her. Karon's gasp of surprise was drowned in the hunger of his mouth.

Tristan slipped his tongue between her parted lips, shocking his system with its first taste of paradise. Her lips, full and sweet, met his as his tongue dueled with hers, saturating his senses with her sweet taste. His hunger for her knew no bounds and when Karon went to pull away, Tristan had to force himself to let her loose. Now that he'd had her in his arms, Tristan wasn't sure if he could let her go.

"Wait, Tristan. The list—"

"I'll fulfill your list and then some."

"But I'm not prepared."

"Perfect," he growled, dragging her back. Karon had been too prepared for too long. It was about damn time something shook up her perfect little world.

Giving in to his demanding kiss, Karon leaned into Tristan,

wrapping her arms around his neck. The curves of her body molded against him, cradling his hard body against her own.

The feel of her, full and thick, forced his cock to jut and his gut to clench. Finally, a woman's body that was meant for a man like him. Soft and supple, as if crafted from a Renoir painting, Karon was the very essence of beauty to him.

Holding her taut against him, Tristan broke away from her mouth, panting with need. "What do you want first, Karon? Should I feel your hungry pussy with my fingers, my mouth or my cock?"

"Do I have to choose?" she questioned, breathless with anticipation.

"No, baby, you don't. There are an infinite number of possibilities that I can't wait to explore."

THREE

OH MY GOD! Laid back with her legs spread and bent at the knees, Karon experienced for the first time in thirty-four years of living, true and utter bliss. She didn't even know when they had made it to his bedroom or when their clothes had slipped into little pools of color and fabric at their feet. All Karon could remember was the hungry look Tristan had sent her seconds before he disappeared between her thighs and began to pleasure her.

Oral sex was amazing. She'd never look at Tristan's mouth the same again. His mouth. His lips. His nimble tongue in all of its naughty glory was driving her quickly out of her mind. Who would have thought that Miss Goody Two-shoes wasn't as good as they thought she was? Not Karon. That was for sure.

Sure, she had heard the jokes. Karon had even laughed at the double entendres that she didn't understand. All in the pretense of the elusive orgasm that was now taking her breath away. Karon hadn't even had the opportunity to suck in her stomach as she had planned. A size sixteen wasn't anything to be too embarrassed about, but she hadn't been looking forward to the first moment of nudity with Tristan. But the second their clothes slid off, he slid between her legs and all thoughts of her size flew out of her mind as his tongue found her heated core.

Gripping the sweat-doused silk sheets in her hands like a lifeline, Karon tried with all of her might not to scream the paint off the walls, but it was hard as hell. The things his tongue was doing were breathtaking, and that thing with his fingers—un-fucking-believable.

She felt as if she were being singed alive, and Karon loved every second of it. In the midst of another orgasm, Tristan moved up from between her splayed thighs and blew gently on her engorged clit.

The chilling breeze sent new tingling sensations coursing through her body. "Good Lord, Tristan," she murmured through parched lips. "Are you trying to kill me?"

"No, just pleasure you, lover."

"I'm pleasured. I'm on pleasure overload." Giggling, Karon dropped her legs limply down on the bed. She wasn't lying. Karon's body was a trembling mound of flesh. Never before had she experienced so much pleasure in one sitting in her entire lifetime. God bless *Blaze Magazine*.

"That's just the start." Moving up over her body, Tristan brushed his ridged length against her quivering, moist center. "I'm thinking we need to move on with the list."

Licking her lips, Karon stared up at Tristan wantonly. "What did you have in mind?"

"Number twenty-two mixed in with a little bit of number nine, followed closely by number five."

Quickly thinking back, Karon tried to remember what the

numbers represented. "You want to have phone sex on a plane while someone is watching us?"

Laughing, Tristan cupped his cock and rubbed the head against her aching clit. Karon moaned as she pushed up against him, desperate to have Tristan finally fill her. In the rain on a train, with a fox in a box, she was through with caring. She just wanted him.

"No, baby, roll over for me." With a final bump of his cock, Tristan sat back on his heels, stroking himself as he waited for her to comply.

She meant to comply. Really she did, but the sight of a handsome man pleasuring himself in front of her was something Karon wasn't about to miss for anything in the world. Hell, it was number three on her list. Karon remembered that number quite well.

"Karon," Tristan called, still pumping his cock between his hands. "Roll over."

"Huh?"

"It's all yours, baby." Encircling the moist head of his cock with his thumb, Tristan moved his finger up to Karon's mouth, coating her bottom lip with his musky flavor. "Number eighteen."

Dashing out her tongue quickly, Karon gathered the juices and savored Tristan's essence. Salty, but not unpleasant. Eyeing his large member, Karon hesitantly reached out for him, brushing Tristan's hand in the process. She had touched a penis before. This part wasn't a novelty to her, but she had never wanted one to be buried deeply inside of her as she did this one. "I want to taste you."

"Not tonight, Karon."

Startled, Karon looked up from her exploring hand and frowned. "Why not?"

"Because I want you too much right now to trust myself in your warm mouth. I'm afraid I'll come too soon and ruin the rest of the night."

"But it's on my list." Even to Karon her voice sounded like a petulant child's. Walter wouldn't let her do it and the few men who had wanted her to, she didn't return the sentiment. But Tristan had agreed and he was hers to do with as she pleased.

"And you will. Trust me, baby, I want your mouth on me just about as much as you want it on me. But another day."

"Another day." Reluctantly releasing his cock, Karon gave it one final stroke before she turned over and lay flat on the bed. "Is this what you wanted?"

"It's a start." Climbing off the bed, Tristan lit a few candles and dimmed the lights. He made a quick stop at his dresser to gather condoms before getting back on the bed with her. "I want you to get up on all fours but then lower your torso back down."

Karon complied, thankful for the darkened room. There was no way she wanted Tristan looking at her huge butt shot straight out like that. She was a bit on the pale side. She didn't want him to go blind.

"What a beautiful sight."

"I doubt it." She snickered, picturing the image in her head.

Rubbing his palms over her bottom, Tristan snorted his disagreement. "Trust me. This is a vision sonnets were written of."

Karon was about to rally with a quip of her own but her breath was stolen once Tristan slid into her waiting body. Hiss-

ing at the unbelievable fullness of him, Karon pressed her face
into the pillow, trying to gather herself.

"Baby, you feel so good," Tristan murmured as he pulled out
and thrust forward again. "So fucking good."

Karon had to disagree. It was he who felt good. His thick
cock stretched and filled her as she had never been filled before.
It was almost too much at times as Tristan powered in and out of
her, but other times it felt as if she'd never get enough.

One man, one night, and she was hooked.

"Look over, Karon," he hoarsely ordered. "Look to the left."

Dragging her head from the pillow, Karon glanced at the
closet doors, which were covered with mirrors. The number
blared in front of her eyes like a red neon light—fourteen. Karon
had said she wanted to watch them have sex. So watch she did.

Tristan pulled back slowly, dragging his hard length almost
completely out of her body before plunging forward again. His
condom-covered cock, slick from her passion, held Karon's attention as it dipped in and out of her hot sex. The vision was sexier than any movie she'd ever seen or any book she'd ever read.

It was the two of them, conjoined. At one with their passion,
and it was mind-blowing.

The image moved her. Unable to resist, Karon began to meet
him thrust for thrust. Slamming back on his cock, fucking him as
he fucked her.

"Now, please, now," she begged, her body tense with need
and ache. Karon's breath was coming in deep, guttural gulps. She
had never felt this way before. An orgasm wasn't something un-
familiar to her, but one so deep and demanding was alien to her.
She wanted to come more than she wanted her next breath.

Driving into her harder, Tristan bent forward and grabbed her hand, placing it between her trembling thighs. "Tease your clit, baby. Strum it and come for me. I want to feel you coming around me."

"Tristan . . ." she cried, rubbing her clit as she pushed back on his cock. She was so close, so fucking close.

"Come for me, baby," Tristan ordered hoarsely, squeezing his hand on the curve of her ass. "Come for me."

Tristan's squeeze brought her over the edge. Karon came in a loud, orgasmic rush, seconds ahead of Tristan, who growled her name as he rode her into the mattress. Karon cried, her body racked with tremors as she held herself up with the last of her waning strength.

Easing out of her, Tristan dropped next to Karon, who was still in the same position they had just made love in. Chuckling, Tristan brushed her damp hair out of her face. "Are you going to lie down?"

"Can't move," she muttered, eyes closed, still enjoying how alive she felt, even though she felt close to death.

Karon felt the bed move as Tristan stood and heard his soft chuckles as he walked across the room. She still didn't move though, just continued to vegetate, lost in her own little orgasmic world.

A cool cloth shocked her back to reality. Opening her eyes, she glanced over her shoulder at a boxers-clad Tristan, who was brushing her body with a damp washcloth. Looking up at her, he smiled. "I think I like you in this position. I'm suddenly feeling the need to get my camera."

His words were all the motivation she needed. Moving

quickly, Karon rolled over and sat up, pulling a pillow to block her flushed body from his view. "That was cruel."

"You are wonderful," he countered, sitting down next to her.

"You're not so bad yourself."

"For a Goody Two-shoes, you're awfully bad."

Blushing, Karon grabbed the pillow next to her and bopped him in the face. "You're never going to let me live that down, are you?"

"Never, especially when we have so many things left on the list to do." Tristan leaned forward and pulled the pillow away from her body. "I have a shower built for two, what do you say we go work on number eleven?"

Okay, it couldn't be that difficult. It was just a penis. All I have to do is lean forward and slip him between my lips.

Quickly glancing at a still-dozing Tristan, Karon wondered if what she was planning was against the law in the state of California. She seriously doubted Tristan would put up much of a fuss if he woke to her giving him head, but if she bit him or did something incredibly wrong, well, that might be a different story altogether.

I'm not going to bite him. I'm not going to bite him. The longer she hesitated, the more apprehensive she became. What the hell was her problem? She had graduated at the top of her class, for Christ's sakes. It was just a penis, a cock, a dick. A penis that was growing increasingly larger before her very eyes.

Eyes widening, Karon reached out tentatively to touch him but drew her hand back quickly when she heard Tristan's rough chuckle.

His erection was standing stiff and proud, pointing toward the ceiling. Tristan was wide awake and watching her with a wicked grin. "Can . . . we help you?"

Sitting up on her heels, Karon frowned down at him. "Go back to sleep. This was much easier when I thought you weren't awake."

"I've been awake for a while, and from the way you were staring at him, it didn't look easy."

"Him. You don't have a name for him . . . I mean your penis?"

"Will personalizing him make it easier for you?"

"Shut up." The underlying challenge in his tone motivated Karon as nothing else would.

Leaning forward, Karon eyed his member again, this time with a hint of greed. Long and thick, the mere sight of his cock had her mouth watering and her once sedate pussy dampening. Karon didn't know if she would be able to fit his entire cock in her mouth but she wanted to give it a try.

Taking his length in her hand, she nervously wet her lips, drawing a chuckle from Tristan. "Don't worry, *baby*, it won't bite," he teased, his voice deep with arousal.

Stroking him, Karon couldn't help but to mutter, "But I might," before taking the last step and sheathing his cock in her mouth. Whatever reply Tristan would have made was lost in his deep groan as she engulfed the head of his thick member.

The feel of him sliding between her lips made Karon feel aroused and powerful all at the same time. Knowing she was in control of his pleasure, even as unskilled as she was, was pleasure in itself.

Karon slid her tongue around the crown of his cock, tasting him as she had never tasted a man before. Her nervous apprehension went away as his groan of approval filled the air. Pushing down, she took as much of his length as she could into her mouth before slowly drawing him back out.

"Fuck, baby," Tristan muttered as she plunged down again, taking his length in as far as her throat would allow. She still wasn't able to swallow his entire length but what she couldn't get in her mouth, she stroked with her hand, sliding the moisture all around his cock.

Giving head wasn't as easy as she'd thought it would be, not that she had thought it would be all that simple, but it involved a lot more hand-eye coordination than she ever would have imagined. Keeping her lips positioned over her teeth wasn't an easy task by far, but Tristan didn't seem to have any complaints, so that had to mean she was doing something right.

Tristan groaned deep in his throat as he wrapped his hand tight in her hair and ordered through gritted teeth, "A little harder, *baby*."

The feel of his hands in her hair released a fresh pool of moisture in her pussy. Groaning around him, Karon tightened her mouth and sucked harder, going with the rhythm Tristan demanded.

"That's so good." Moving his hips up, he pushed deeper in her throat, moaning as her teeth lightly scraped him.

Karon pulled back with a groan, unsure whether or not she had hurt him. "I'm so sorry."

Pushing her back toward his throbbing cock, Tristan slid back into her mouth. "Don't be sorry, do it again. A little pain can be a good thing."

Tristan guided her in a motion that soon had him arching his back.

"Pull back, baby. I'm about to come," Tristan warned as the orgasm coursed through him. Karon refused to move. She hadn't come this far for nothing. Bracing herself for the unknown flavor of him full force, Karon tightened her grip, pumping quicker as she sucked harder, relishing in his pleasure as he came with a gush in her mouth.

Oh my God! His fluid flooded her mouth, almost gagging Karon. But she swallowed, chatting to herself the entire time. *Don't throw up. You'll never be able to forgive yourself. Just swallow.*

And with her pep talk in her head, she did.

When Tristan released her hair, Karon took her mouth from around his cock and dropped back on her heels as proud of herself as when she'd passed her real-estate exams. She had given head. Done a damn fine job of it, if she said so herself. The best part was, she hadn't thrown up.

Semen was slimy, saltier than a pretzel, but not the worst thing she'd ever had in her mouth. Clams were worse by far. But the point was, she knew from firsthand experience how semen tasted. Happy early birthday to her.

Tristan let out a satisfying groan as his wet cock twitched against his stomach. "I don't know if I should applaud or just pass out."

"So you liked?"

Tristan held his hand out to her and pulled her down to him. "No, *baby*, I loved."

"Great. Uh . . . Tristan?"

"Yes?"

"Can I have a drink of water?"

MINDFUL OF THE TIME, Tristan turned the headlights out on his car as he parked it in front of Karon's house, but kept the engine running. It was a bit cooler tonight than he'd hoped for, but he wasn't going to let the weather ruin his plans.

They were two weeks into *the* list and Tristan was having the time of his life. If he'd known that under all those proper suits and behind her killer smile there was wanton with energy to spare, he would have attacked Karon years ago and claimed her, man or no man.

Tristan was having just as much fun thinking of new ways to fulfill her fantasies as he was making love with her. Karon was remarkable and he couldn't wait to see how she would react to his latest plan.

With a smile, he dialed her number from memory as he adjusted the driver's-side seat. He wanted to be as comfortable as possible when he marked number ten off the list. Just saying *the* list made Tristan want to laugh. Despite the fact that they were checking things off faster than Santa on speed, Karon still refused to call it *her* list. It was just one more thing he adored about her.

As he hit send on his cell phone, Tristan looked toward her darkened house. Her car was parked in the driveway so he knew she was home. Now all he had to do was get her to answer the phone. Tristan was hoping she'd be in bed, or at least about to go to bed.

"Hello."

"What are you wearing?"

There was a short pause before she answered back, "Tristan, is that you?"

"If I answer your question, will you answer mine?"

"You are so crazy." She laughed softly.

"No, I'm hard. Now tell me, what are you wearing?"

"What am I . . . ?" Tristan could tell the exact moment Karon realized what was going on. Her voice went from light and cheery to a sudden halt, followed quickly by a continuous flood-gate of "Ohhhhh boyyyy."

He was thankful Karon couldn't see his face right now because he was more than sure his large grin would only cause her rambling to go on longer than need be. "It's a simple question, baby, what are you wearing?"

A loud whooshing sound filled the line as if Karon had let out a deep breath. "If you would have told me we were going to do number ten, I would have prepared. My legs aren't shaved, my hair is a mess and I have on an ugly old jersey."

"A jersey, huh." Choosing to weed through all of her jumble, Tristan focused on the one tidbit he was interested in. "What color is it? How much does it cover?"

"It's black and goes down to the middle of my thighs."

"Is that all?"

"Yes." Her tone had softened. "I just got out of the shower. Actually, I'm still a bit moist. The shirt is clinging to me everywhere."

Leaning back in his seat, Tristan closed his eyes, envisioning Karon standing before him, dressed as she'd described. The athlete in him had a thing for girls in jerseys, especially when they weren't wearing much else. "You sound beautiful."

"You sound horny."

"Thanks to you, it's a state I know well."

"Just me?"

Tristan could hear the question in her voice. She really didn't know just how damn beautiful she was. "Just you, baby. I want to play with only you. Speaking of playing . . . "

"Yes?"

"Do you have any toys?"

"Toys?" She gasped.

"Yes, toys of the sexual variety."

"Ohh . . . " Tristan could swear he heard her blush. "A few."

"Perfect. I want you to go to your bedroom and climb on the bed with your favorite one."

"Tristan, I feel stupid doing this. Maybe this was a silly thing to add to *the* list."

"I don't think it's silly."

"You don't?"

Far from it. "A hard-on this fierce has absolutely nothing to do with silliness."

"Hard . . . on?"

Tristan tightened his hand around the bulge protruding from his pants, adding just enough pressure to send shivers down his spine. This wasn't just for Karon. He was doing this for himself as well. Ever since he'd read her list, he'd been fixated on making sure he made every single thing she wanted come true. It didn't even feel like a goal anymore, more like a mission. "My cock is hard for you. Just you. It's your hands I'm imagining stroking me, your mouth I want to shoot my load in. It's all about you."

"Tristan, you should come with a warning label."

"I just want to come with you." Tristan released his grip on his cock. "Did you get the toy?"

Karon hesitated for a second before answering, "Yes."

"What is it?"

"A vibrator."

"What does it look like?"

"It's pink and shaped like a penis, with ridges and a large head."

Tristan rested the phone between his shoulder blade and his ear, so he could quickly unbuckle his pants. His plan didn't call for him to come but he never said he wouldn't enjoy this as much as possible. Freeing his member into his waiting hand, Tristan pumped a few times, needing to relieve some of the built-up stress. "Listen to what I want you to do."

"Okay."

"Don't think of this as a toy. Think of it as my cock. The cock you love to fuck and suck. Do you have the image in your head?"

"Yes." Her answer could only be classified as a whimper. It looked as if she was enjoying this as much as he was.

"Now, if that was my cock in your hand, what would you do to him?"

"I'd take him into my mouth."

"That's right, baby. Suck my cock. Run your tongue up and down my length. Make daddy feel good to be home."

The loud slurping sound was answer enough. Tristan shivered

as he tried to imagine what Karon must look like. Her pretty mouth filled with cock, her face flushed with desire.

Fuck, he wanted to come in.

After several painful seconds when Tristan thought he'd lose his mind listening to her pleasure the toy, he decided to move forward. "That's enough, baby. Do you have him all nice and wet?"

"Yes."

"Is he the only thing all nice wet?"

"No, I'm wet. I want you to come here and fuck me."

"Oh, I am there, baby. I'm in your hands. Don't you remember?"

"Tristan, I want you."

Now, those were words he'd never tire of hearing. "And I want you too, but right now what I want most is for you to lie back and spread those sexy little legs of yours wide. Then I want you to take my cock and put him on vibration mode and slip him around your wet pussy."

"Gawd . . . " she whimpered sultrily, a sound so hot it shot straight to his soul. His dirty little angel was fucking herself as he pumped himself. Could it get much better than this?

"Tease your clit, baby. Rub my cock around your pretty little bud."

Whimpering, she let out a little moan, one that caused Tristan to grasp his cock harder and let out a little moan of his own.

"Tell me what you're doing, baby. And tell me using words you know I want to hear."

"I'm fucking myself with your cock." Her Southern accent made the words sound even dirtier. "It's inside me. So deep." She breathed into the phone, her sexy tone causing his cock to jerk in his hands. If Tristan wasn't careful, he was going to come and ruin everything else he had planned for the night.

"Don't just leave it in, baby. Pull him out, then pump him back in. Fuck the cock like it's an extension of mine. Fuck your sweet, juicy pussy."

"Tristan, Triss . . . " Unable to finish the sentence, Karon's cries of passion resonated through the phone line. She was going to come. Hell, she was coming and Tristan wanted to watch.

Turning off the car, Tristan shoved his very hard and aching cock back into his pants before he bolted out of the car. He barely remembered to lock it behind him as he took off for her front door with one end in mind. He had a pussy to reclaim and an ass to possess.

FOUR

*T*RISTAN WAS TRYING TO KILL HER. Still clutching the phone in her trembling fingers, Karon tried hard to get her breathing back under control. Phone sex was the last thing she'd been expecting to do tonight, but damn, it was fun.

Limp and sedated, Karon dropped the still-vibrating toy on the floor and rolled over onto her side. "In a word . . . "

"Yes?"

"Wow." Even that didn't say quite enough. "Can I just compliment you on your . . . phone skills?"

Tristan's chuckle made her smile. Then again, everything about him made her smile. He was addictive and too damn adorable for her peace of mind. "I'm glad you approve but the night isn't over yet."

"You didn't come?"

"No, I'm saving it all for you."

Karon liked the sound of that. "Are you ready for round two, then?"

"Three and four as well."

"What do you want me to do now?" Karon eyed the damp toy, wondering what Tristan had in store for her next.

"You can start by opening your door."

Startled, Karon sat up straight as her doorbell rang. He was there! Really there!

"OhmyGawd! OhmyGawd!" Jumping out of the bed, Karon stared toward the door as if she expected him to walk in at any moment. It was ridiculous of course; Tristan didn't have a key, but then again, he wasn't supposed to be at her house when she looked like this.

"Let me in, Karon."

"No, you have to come back in an hour, after I've combed my hair and shaved."

"I'm not going anywhere. Let me in."

"But, Tristan . . . " Even as she protested, Karon stumbled down the hall to do his bidding. It served him right to see her out of sorts.

"The only butt I'm concerned with right this second is your own. Now let me in."

Grumbling, Karon clicked her phone off and tossed it on the couch as she passed by. When she reached the front door, she quickly unlocked and opened it, intent on telling him off, but as soon as she swung open the door, her plan went right out the door.

Tristan was over her threshold before she even prepared her spiel. Taking her in his arms, he pushed her back until she was flat against the wall and he was leaning into her, hard cock and all.

Licking her lips nervously, Karon stared into his passion-filled eyes and forgot why she ever felt the need to complain about him being there in the first place.

"Is that an offer, baby?"

"Wh-what?"

"You're licking your lips like you want something between them." Tristan leaned forward and nipped at her bottom lip gently before moving to her neck, where he continued to drive her mad. "Do you, baby?"

She hadn't until he mentioned it, but now that he did . . . "Yes."

Tristan moved his hip into her, pressing his erection in the apex of her thighs. Clutching at his T-shirt, Karon moved against him, impatient to have his cock inside of her. If he wanted her to suck him, she would. Right now, she didn't care where he fucked her as long as he did.

"I would love," Tristan dragged out the word *love* until it felt like a caress against her skin, "for you to take me in your sweet mouth. Your lips and your tongue are a close second to your hot, tight pussy."

"Hmm, that sounds good." Karon started to drop to her knees but Tristan held her upright. She frowned in confusion.

"As good as your mouth sounds, I have other plans in mind." Tristan palmed her ass, bare under her jersey. "Although number ten was very, very good, I want to try out number four."

Karon's eyes widened as Tristan slid his finger down the crease of her ass. "Ahh, wasn't it on the maybe list?"

"No, but just let me give you my best reason why it's on my *to-do* list." Tristan slapped her ass lightly and Karon blushed with the realization that she was getting wet all over again at the thought of him taking her ass. She had turned into a total freak and she loved every minute of it.

"Someone's thinking dirty thoughts." Tristan tilted her head back as his hand slipped between her thighs. "I think you *like* the idea."

"Maybe . . ."

"No maybe about it." Spanking her ass again, he turned and quickly hustled her back toward her bedroom.

Karon wasn't sure if she should be nervous or excited. The thought of him buried in her backside had her tingling, but the exact how and ow made her apprehensive.

Standing in front of her bed, Karon wondered what precisely she was supposed to do. Was there a proper anal protocol she didn't know about? Did she get up on her knees or lay on her back?

Damn it. She didn't have a clue what to do next.

"Stop thinking so hard." Tristan slipped up behind her, hugging her to him.

"I don't know if that's possible."

"Do you trust me?"

Karon answered with no hesitation. "Yes."

"Then trust me to know how to please you." Tristan gripped the edge of her jersey and pulled it off, dropping it to the floor behind her.

Instinctively, Karon sucked in her stomach. She couldn't help it. Even after all this time, she still wasn't comfortable being nude with him. "Get on the bed and lie on your side."

Instructions, now that was what she needed. Quickly moving to the bed, Karon lay down and faced him. "Now what?"

"I brought you a present." Tristan pulled a small tube out of his pocket and tossed it on the bed next to Karon.

Confused, Karon looked down at the white tube, turning it over so she could read the label. "K-Y Jelly." Eyes wide, she turned back to look at Tristan, who was grinning down at her. "Is lube the new candle?"

Tristan laughed as he pulled his T-shirt over his head. "It's the gift that keeps on giving."

As usual, the second Tristan started to undress, Karon lost track of everything else. It was still a bit mind-boggling to her that a man who looked as good as he did would be interested in a woman who looked as ordinary as she did. Apparently karma worked after all.

"Do you like what you see?" Tristan winked as he dropped his pants to the floor.

Karon eyed his erection hungrily. "I do now."

"Roll over on your back."

"You just had me turn on my side."

"Only so I could watch you as I undressed."

"Pervert," she teased as she complied.

"You got a problem with that?" Grasping her ankle, Tristan opened her legs to his gaze. She could practically feel the heat from his burning stare.

"Are you going to keep looking at me all night or what?"

Chuckling, Tristan knelt between her legs. "Eager little thing, aren't you?"

Karon didn't feel the need to answer aloud. The proof was right in front of him, in the form of her very moist pussy. "Looks like somebody had a little fun on the phone."

"Just a bit."

"Only a bit." Tristan slid his hand down her thigh, grazing his fingers across her puffy lips. "Let's see if I can move it up to a lot."

Karon arched her hips hungrily, not caring if she looked like some sort of lust-crazed woman. She had become addicted to Tristan and didn't care if she was ever cured. Of course, it didn't seem as if he minded too much. He appeared to appreciate her enthusiastic displays.

"That's right, baby, open up for me." Tristan bent his head, lapping at her cream like a kitten. Swirling his tongue around her clit, he drove her insane with his mouth.

Tristan feasted between her legs, spurring Karon on with his oral talent. Just as her body tightened up in anticipation of her release, he surprised her by moving his tongue from her aching, wet pussy to her tight rosette.

"Ohh . . . " she whimpered, her eyes closing tightly as the new sensations washed over her.

His tongue was touching her . . . oh my Gawd, it felt good. Karon dug her nails into the bed, trying to control her gyrating hips from bucking up into his face. She never would have thought, never dreamt something so dirty could ever feel so good.

Pleasure rippled over her skin, like a soft rainfall. Her nipples begged for his touch. Her pussy cried out to be filled, but Tristan was on an agenda of his own. He lapped at her nether hole until Karon thought she'd go mad.

"Tristan . . . please."

Tristan answered her plea, but not in the way Karon expected. Instead of moving away from her, he added his fingers to his wicked torture. Circling her slick rosette, he eased his way into her body.

"Oh, fuck, yes."

"Is this what you've been waiting for?" Tristan pushed his finger in and out of her tight hole as Karon tried to stay as still as possible.

It was an impossible goal though, because despite what her spirit wanted to do, her body had a will of its own. Karon began to move under his touch, taking his finger deeper and deeper with every stroke.

"Do you like the way this feels?"

"Yes," she murmured, turning away from his lustful gaze. Even though anal sex had been on her list, Karon still felt naughty for wanting to experience the backdoor pleasure. It seemed so taboo, yet she didn't want him to stop.

It was the most bizarre feeling in the world, yet the sensation was pleasurable at the same time.

Tristan slowly penetrated her tight opening, stretching her one finger width at a time. He kept up the steady pace, adding a second then a third finger, priming her until she was taking him in deeper and easier every time.

Karon's body was on fire, and she felt stretched and filled as she'd never been before. Just when she thought she couldn't take a second more of the maddening pleasure, Tristan pulled his fingers out of her tight sheath.

Grabbing the tube from the bed, he quickly coated his cock with a mixture of the jelly and her juices. Tristan stroked himself a few times before moving back between her spread legs.

"Are you ready, baby?" His voice sounded strained, as if she wasn't the only one in need. "When I push in, I want you to push out."

Karon wanted to call out for him to wait, but the words never made it past her lips as the thick head of his cock pressed against her entrance. Closing her eyes, she arched her back, pushing out as Tristan had ordered her. Karon cried out in a mingling of pleasure and pain as he eased the crown of his cock past her resisting ring.

There was a brief twinge of pain, a full, heated sensation that spread quickly like a brush fire. Yet it wasn't overwhelming or entirely painful, more like incredibly full. Karon felt stretched and more aroused than she could ever remember being in her life.

Tristan had claimed her, in a way no man had done before. He was deep inside of her and it was wonderful.

"Fuck, baby, you feel so good. So fucking good." Tristan pulled his hips back slowly before pushing forward once more. "Tell me it's good for you."

"Good," she muttered hungrily, moving her hands up to her breasts to squeeze her aroused nipples, needing more than just the anal stimulation. She was so close, so close. "Just don't stop."

Tristan laughed hoarsely as he pumped inside of her. "Don't worry, love, that will never happen."

Karon moaned in approval, unable to do much else.

As if he sensed in her a need for more stimulation, Tristan pulled her hands down to her pussy, urging her silently to tease her erect bud. Karon didn't need a set of instructions for this. Frigging her clit furiously, Karon worked her body over quickly as she met him thrust for thrust, loving the way he felt powering into her.

"That's it, baby, fuck your juicy pussy," Tristan growled, pumping faster into her ass.

His dirty words and sawing hips were the trigger to her orgasm. Crying out his name, Karon came, seconds ahead of Tristan's own powerful release.

"Fuck. So good . . . so good," he groaned as he pushed for a final thrust, pumping his seed inside her waiting ass. "Mine . . . mine . . . "

Karon couldn't have agreed more. He was so good, and she was completely his.

"THIS LITTLE ANNOYING SMILE of yours, will it be going away anytime soon?"

Tristan looked up past the bar he'd been lifting to stare up into his best friend and business partner Lucas Holmes's sweaty face. "It's hit me, man."

"Damn." Standing up straight from his crouch, Lucas shook his head in disgust. "Not you too."

"Sorry, old man," Tristan teased as he brought the weights down toward his chest before pushing them upward toward Lucas, who was spotting him. "But I think she might be the one."

"The one." Lucas snorted as he got back into position. "There's no such thing as the one. There's the one you're going to take home tonight. Or the one you're going to sneak out of bed with tomorrow. Those are the only 'ones' I ever want to hear you referring to."

"Then you better close your ears." Struggling with the

last rep, Tristan paused between his words as he gathered his strength to push the weights up to Lucas's waiting hands.

"I got it." With the ease of a man who was comfortable around weights and working out, Lucas grasped the bar and pulled it up. After setting the weights back in their rightful positions, he grabbed the damp towel and dropped it down onto Tristan's upturned face.

Feeling too good to care, Tristan just chuckled as he mopped his brow. He and Lucas were the last two holdouts, as they liked to refer to themselves. The last two single men from their fraternity, but if things kept going as great as they were with Karon, Lucas would be the lone holdout.

Ducking from underneath the bar, Tristan sat up and winced as his muscles throbbed beneath his skin. He was pushing too hard. They were getting way too old for this shit. It was one thing to try to stay in shape and a complete other to push the envelope for the sake of garnering female attention.

The only attention Tristan wanted was from Karon, and since their first night together, he'd been getting it in spades. As far as he was concerned, they had moved from teacher to lover in a single night. This thing, whatever it was between them, wasn't just about sex.

Sure, there was lots of sex. Lots of hot, dirty, rough sex, like last night's bout of sexual deviant delight.

It had started out easy enough—a bed, two neckties and a blindfold. In all truth, Tristan had placed those items there as a little joke. To tease his little sheltered seductress. The joke had been on him though, because not only had Karon's eyes lit up at the sight of them, she also eagerly climbed onto the bed and began to stroke the tie seductively.

The fire in her eyes should have set off a little warning bell that things weren't exactly as they had seemed. And thanks to some very persuasive oral sex, Tristan ended up tied and blindfolded for Karon's pleasure.

Not that he had much reason to complain. Her pleasure was his pleasure and she'd kept him at the brink all night long. When she was finally ready for her own pleasure, Karon proudly climbed on top of his cock, sinking ever so slowly down his rigid length.

Once her tight sheath had enveloped him in her warmth, Tristan had had enough. Ruining perfectly good ties, he had ripped them off the headboard and used the tattered remains to bind her hands above her head as he switched positions, placing her on the bottom for his time to be in charge.

Bondage had quickly gone from the maybe section of her list to the 'oh baby' section of her list.

Nights like that were wonderful, but then there were times that they didn't have sex at all. Sometimes they would just spend time with each other, watching movies or talking over dinner. Little things that were all adding up, one day at a time.

Tristan never thought it would be possible to be this happy and content with just one woman, but Karon was special. He'd always thought so, but now he knew it to be fact. She had a way of making everyone around her feel a hundred feet tall. Just being with Karon in general made him feel like a better person.

If he didn't know any better, he'd say he was falling for her.

Hell, he knew better. He was falling for her. All in the space of a few weeks. It was unbelievable. But it was true.

"If you don't stop it, I'm seriously going to have to kick your ass."

Chuckling, Tristan swung his towel around his neck. "Then you'd wake up."

"Get up." Lucas swatted Tristan with his towel. Before lying back, Lucas ran his towel over the bench. Settling his feet on the floor, he brought his hands up under the bar and, with Tristan's help, pushed up before bringing the weights down to his muscular chest. "I'll give it a week."

"It's already been three." Tristan watched over him, watching for any signs of strain. Ready at a moment's notice to grab the weight if it became too much for Lucas to handle.

Not that it would. Lucas worked out at least five times a week, dragging Tristan with him as often as he could. Gone was the wiry frame his friend had had in college, in its place was a muscle-packed body Lucas gladly primped on command.

Lucas was a proud narcissist and one of Tristan's best friends.

"You won't last three more," Lucas countered between thrusts.

"And which ex-girlfriend are you holding a grudge against this week?"

"Pick one." He laughed as he pressed the weight up.

"One good word for you, buddy. Therapy."

"I can't go back there anymore. She won't counsel me now that I fucked her sister."

Tristan shook his head in bemusement. "See . . . there's something very wrong with you."

"That's what she said."

Ignoring Lucas's comment, Tristan leaned forward to help with the bar. "Give me three more."

"I'll give you three reasons it won't last." As he pushed up, he counted off. "One, you aren't the settling-down type. Two, if she's dating you, she is the settling-down type because she sees how much money you make. Three, her vapidness will bore you."

"One." Tristan grabbed the bar and placed it back in its holder. "You don't have a clue what type I am. Two, I think she makes more money than I do. And three, Karon isn't stupid."

"Karon . . . " Squinting, Lucas stared at him as if he were try-ing to place the name. "Not Bower Real Estate Karon?"

"The very one," Tristan said with pride.

Lucas's eyes were wide with surprise. "She's not the sort . . . you normally go for."

"Why do you say that?" Amusement gone, Tristan waited for Lucas's next words. He'd hate like hell to have to beat the shit out of Lucas, but he would if he said anything that he thought was the slightest bit out of line.

"She seems . . . almost too smart to go out with a guy like you." At Tristan's snort, Lucas continued. "A little plumper than I normally like, but it looks like it's all in the right places."

"Don't think too hard on it." Tristan didn't like the idea that Lucas had thought about Karon at all. "And don't call her plump. She's beautiful."

"Right pretty girl, that's for sure." A teasing glint was in his eyes. "You don't have to get so sissified over it."

"I didn't get sissified."

"See what *potential* love does to you?" Sitting up, Lucas wiped his brow as he moved off the bench. As he stood up, he dropped the towel around his neck and nodded to a pretty, petite blonde who was walking by them, eyeing them with a killer come-hither look. "Now take, for example, that lovely lady."

"I don't want to take her."

"Fine, I will, but later. She's not really here to work out."

Tristan sat down on the rowing machine and grasped the bars in his hands. Looking over his shoulder at the lady in question, he shook his head in amusement and faced forward again to begin his strokes.

"What was your first hint?" he asked as Lucas joined him on the machine next to him. "The makeup? Or the dry towel?"

"The fact that she's walked past us three times in the last fifteen minutes, and that's what makes her perfect."

"For you maybe."

"You too not so long ago," Lucas grumbled. "Why now? We're in the prime of our lives. We make good money. We look great, me more so than you, and it's only going to get better with age. Why would you want to give all of that up for the same tail every night?"

Tristan didn't know why he had never noticed it before, but Lucas was a big-ass titty baby. "Are you listening to yourself, man? You call me sissified."

"I'm trying to save you from a big mistake."

Tristan didn't believe that for a second. "No, you're trying to save yourself from hitting the clubs by yourself. Doesn't it get old?"

"Never," Lucas drawled as he grinned leeringly. "But you'll see. This infatuation of yours won't last."

"I think you're the one who's infatuated. Next thing you know you'll be asking me if you look fat in that outfit." *Infatuation* wasn't even the right word for what he was feeling for Karon but he wasn't going to share that tidbit with Lucas. His friend didn't look as if he was going to shut up anytime soon as it was and

Tristan didn't want to give him more material. "Just leave me to my bliss and I'll leave you to your ignorance."

"Your bliss is annoying. You're acting like one of those smiling la, la, la fucking little dwarfs." Lucas shivered as if in distaste. "It's maddening."

"I'm sorry if my happiness is bothering you." Tristan snorted, fighting to hold his smile back. "I'll try to be more down-spirited when I'm around you."

"I'd appreciate it, and that's all I'm going to say on the matter." His pact of silence lasted less than a second. "You know, monogamy is contagious. I don't want to wake up tomorrow feeling the need to settle down."

Tristan burst out laughing. Stopping in mid stroke, he turned to his friend, who was grinning like a loon. "Lucas, the only thing you're going to catch is a statutory rape lawsuit."

Lucas looked back fondly toward the girl, who was now lingering near the water fountain. "No worries, she's over eighteen."

"Barely." Tristan eyed her, unconvinced. She was cute, but she had trouble written all over her.

"You don't get arrested for *barely*."

And that was probably all that mattered to him. "Man, you have serious issues."

"Don't I know it?"

"One of these days, you're going to meet a woman who is going to make you change your tune."

Lucas looked aghast at the notion. "Now you're just being mean."

FIVE

HE MUSIC PUMPING over the loudspeakers was just the motivation Karon needed to keep up her flow on the treadmill. Six miles and going strong. She had hardly broken a sweat. Karon was in the zone.

Working out had never felt so rewarding. Neither had gym day. For the first time Karon had something to gossip with her friends about, and they were enthralled by her new and improved sex life.

Seven miles and she wasn't ready to quit. Today was turning out to be a new record kind of a day. It was amazing how a little sex, okay, who was she kidding, a lot of sex, got a girl's motor going.

"I hate you both," Zoya panted, giving up the pretense of even walking anymore. The plump brunette was leaning on the machine as if it were a lifeline. "The one freaking lunch date I miss in three years, Karon decides to come out of the freak closet."

"I'm not a freak." Karon grinned, although some of the things she and Tristan had done over the last three weeks were definitely putting her in line for runner-up. "I'm a liberated woman in the prime of my sexual peak."

"Amen." Jacque threw her arms up in the air comically. "Preach, sister."

"Look at her. She's glowing, for Pete's sake." Wiping her brow, Zoya watched Karon in awe. "So did you finish the list?"

"I might have, if Tristan didn't keep insisting on adding to it."

"Adding to it?" Hitting the stop button on the machine, Jacque grasped her sides as she tried to catch her breath. "I didn't think we left anything out."

Ending her session as well, Karon stepped down, wiping the handles with her towel for the next person. "Apparently we did."

"Well, go 'head then," teased Jacque.

"Wait." Zoya looked between Jacque and Karon like they had lost their collective minds. "Am I the only person who thinks this is going to end badly?"

Jacque and Karon turned twin expressions of annoyance in Zoya's direction, causing her to throw up her hands in mock surrender. Karon didn't want to hear about things ending, badly or otherwise. For the first time she wasn't putting her career first. She was going to enjoy it, whether she was supposed to or not.

"All I'm saying is, you can't base a relationship on a booty call."

"Maybe she doesn't want a relationship."

"Of course she does, Jacque, she's not like you."

"What the heck does that mean?"

Karon stifled a chuckle. She knew what Zoya meant, but like always, her friend spoke first and thought second. "Oh, shut up, you know what I meant. Karon is more cautious and too kind-hearted for her own good. I mean, who else would have put up with Walter for that long?"

Rolling her eyes, Jacque held up her hand, signaling for Zoya to shut up. "Move on. There's nothing wrong with not thinking things out."

Zoya batted Jacque's hand with her damp towel. "That should be your motto."

"It is."

"Ladies." Karon shook her head in amusement. After seven years of friendship, it was amusing how well defined their roles were. Karon was the levelheaded peacekeeper of the group, Jacque was the outgoing flirt and Zoya was the ball-breaker. They were each other's support and family. Like family, they tended to be too honest at times. "I'm not looking for this to become a relationship. I'm just going to enjoy Tristan for as long as possible."

"Then toss him back for a younger model."

"Cradle robber," Zoya teased. Jacque had a thing about younger men and it was an ongoing joke between the friends.

"Hey, if you can't find a man, raise one."

"See, that's just wrong and why you're going to end up arrested for hanging out in front of the high schools."

Jacque paused in mid stride. "Hey, maybe I should make a list."

"Oh brother," Karon groaned. She should have known Jacque would take it this far. Jacque could never leave well enough alone.

"See what you started," Zoya moaned as if reading her thoughts.

"I can see it now." Spreading her hands up in the air in front of her, Jacque continued, "Younger Man Wanted. Must be old enough to vote, but not old enough to drink. Must be horny, eager and willing to please. Boys with chest hair need not apply."

Bursting out laughing, Karon looked over at Zoya, who was having a hard time keeping a straight face. "You're insane." Looking back at Karon, Zoya asked, "So do you really think you can keep this up and not get emotionally attached?"

"I don't know." Karon would never admit to Zoya that she was already becoming emotionally attached. She really enjoyed being with Tristan but she didn't think he was the settling-down type and she didn't want to blow it by making demands of him. Karon was just going to have to sit back and enjoy him for as long as she could. Then worry about her heart later.

"Now isn't this a pleasant surprise?"

With a squeal, Karon spun around and stared into the very eyes of the man she had been bragging about. "Tristan, what are you doing here?"

Zoya's snort of amusement warned Karon how silly her question sounded the second she uttered it.

But Tristan, kind soul that he was, refrained from pointing out the obvious. "I didn't know you came here."

Still reeling from seeing him so soon after speaking of him in a very frank and naughty manner, Karon was rattled. She instantly went on the defense. "It may not look like it, but I try to get in to work out once or twice a week."

"That's not what I was implying, Karon." Tristan's tone had lost some of its friendliness. "We've already discussed how pleasing I find your current form."

"Pleasing . . . I think I might like you." Jacque butted in, moving closer to them as she made the much-appreciated effort to shut up her friend. "We haven't been formally introduced."

Tristan took her hand into his and shook it warmly. "But the impression you made was lasting, I assure you. Karon, isn't it?"

Batting his arm teasingly, Jacque lowered her gaze coyly. "You're not getting me this time, Tristan. I'm on to you."

Pettiness rose up inside Karon as she watched Jacque flirt with Tristan. She knew of course that it was just Jacque's way, but for the first time in their friendship, she wanted to push her friend into a vat of ice cream and force her to eat her way out.

"If you two are done being overly nice, I'm Zoya, the other friend."

Karon threw Zoya a "thank you" look, which was cut short by Jacque, who strolled in front of Karon, rolling her eyes as she moved out of the way so Zoya could meet Tristan.

"I just want you to know that if I had been at lunch that day, none of this would have occurred."

"Really . . . then I have to say that I'm awfully pleased you weren't there."

Zoya's startled gaze sent Karon diving for her towel to cover the grin that was threatening to split her face wide open. Not many people stood up to her brazen friend and Tristan did it without even trying.

Jacque, on the other hand, didn't feel a need to hide her amusement. "Back up, Attila, give the man some room."

"Room for you to gush over him." Zoya tossed her sweaty towel at her friend with a grin of her own.

"Ladies, ladies, ladies," a masculine voice called from behind them.

Karon turned around to see who the newest intruder was on girls' day out. When she recognized the face of Tristan's partner Lucas, she smiled warmly.

Karon had a little soft spot for Lucas. He had this wonderful ability to be charming like a snake one second and completely kidlike the next. She could easily see why these two men were friends.

"Who are you?" Zoya rudely asked, being ruder than normal, even for her.

"What she really meant to say"—Jacque stepped forward, bumping Zoya out of the way—"was hi, her name is Zoya and you are?"

Zoya's narrowed gaze did not bode well for future get-togethers.

"Everyone, this is Tristan's business partner—"

"And friend," Lucas added, holding out his hand charmingly to Jacque. When she clasped hands with him, he twisted his wrist and bent forward to kiss the back of her hand. "Lucas Holmes."

"Charmed, I'm sure." Jacque turned up the heat, sending Lucas a flash from her sixty-watt smile.

"I'm going to be sick," Zoya muttered under her breath. "Heading to the kickboxing class."

"You're not really going to take that class, are you?" Lucas's surprise was extremely evident in his voice.

"Take it, no. I teach it."

Lucas's eyes wandered down her sweaty, plump body, lingering over her breasts before meeting her gaze.

The long appraisal set Zoya off. Crossing her arms over her bountiful chest, she faced him head-on, not mindful of the fact that he could more than likely pick her up by the top of her head and dunk her into the nearest trash can. "Did you get your fill?"

"Not really, but I think I'll go take your class to drink in more of your . . . charm."

"You can't handle my class, boy."

"I'm sorry, *Smurfette*, I didn't quite hear you."

Karon faked a cough into her towel to try and cover the sound of the laughter that was bubbling up inside of her. Lucas was in for a world of trouble, he just didn't know it yet.

Tristan spoke softly as he leaned in close to her. "Twenty on Lucas."

With a smile, Karon shook her head. "Kiss that money good-bye, baby."

"Oh yeah." Jacque walked up next to Karon, eyes wide as she watched Lucas and Zoya head down the aisle toward the mirror-filled room. "She's going to rip him a new one. Pity. He's kind of cute."

"He won't be when she's done with him," Karon teased.

"This I have to see."

"You know, that's a good idea. Why don't you go down there and watch the show of all shows while I get cleaned up?" Karon stepped back, smiling at her brilliant plan. By the time Zoya kicked Lucas's butt all over the room, she'd be dressed, made up and ready for Tristan to look at her.

"Hey, wait a minute." Tristan's brow was creased with a frown. "Where are you going?"

"To get cleaned up." Tristan didn't know how hard it was for her to continue talking to him when he looked so good and she looked so bad. Men could work out for hours and walk away looking like a wet dream come to life.

Karon had been fighting the urge since he walked over to grab her towel and throw it over her face so he wouldn't be able to look at her. Dressed in bulky sweats and a perspiration-dampened, clingy T-shirt made her feel more exposed than when she was naked underneath him. At least then, she had makeup to cover up the things the soft light let through. Here, under the harsh beam of gym lights, she was sure she looked like death warmed over.

"Are you done working out?"

"Yes." She wasn't Zoya or Jacque. An hour was enough for her.

Tristan pulled off the towel that had been wrapped around his neck and brought it up to pat her face gently. "Then how about you and I go get a bite of dinner?"

"That sounds fun." As long as she could shower, she was up for anything.

"Great. I'll wait outside the changing room for you."

"You don't have to do that." How sweet.

"I want to do that. Just like I would love to spend the rest of the evening standing here basking in your glow."

Wiping at her forehead in disgust, Karon sighed. "Don't you mean drowning in my sweat?"

"You say potato—"

"You're too much."

"And I'd say . . . you're just enough." With a smile, Tristan pulled her close to him and kissed her gently on the lips. "See you in thirty minutes."

"Okay." Karon watched him walk away, noticing the stares he was getting from women working out. Unable to resist, she walked right down the aisle that he had walked down and said to the many women who were still staring after him, "Yes, girls, he's mine." Their looks of surprise kept her amused all the way to the changing room.

"WHEN YOU SAID DINNER and a movie, I think I was expecting something a bit more—"

"Formal?" Tristan asked around a mouthful of hot dog.

"Exactly."

Karon smiled as he asked, taking the napkin off her lap to wipe at the mustard on his chin. She might not have been expecting a drive-in movie when he picked her up this evening but she seemed as if she was enjoying it.

When Tristan had seen that Phillips Cinema Drive-In was doing a revival of classic horror movies, he instantly knew that this was the place to take Karon for her number six.

Besides, if they were going to have sex in a car, then they were going to do it old-school and in style. It was as if the makers of Lexus instinctively made the luxury car for backseat loving. Roomy, with leather interior to prevent stains, it was made for drive-in lovefests.

Looking around at the other cars pulled in next to theirs with the windows rolled down to hold the speaker box, Tristan felt a sense of nostalgia. And from the looks of the many classic cars filling the lot, he wasn't the only one. The three-day revival had drawn more people closer to their age than it had teenagers, which would make the backseat tango a little less embarrassing. Sex in a car was illegal, but here it was a bit more acceptable.

"*The Blob*." Shaking her head, Karon grinned over at Tristan. "This is too much. Just when I think I have you figured out, you go and surprise me."

"I have to make sure I'm keeping your attention."

"Oh, you have it, all right." Leaning over the center console, Karon surprised Tristan by pressing a quick kiss to his cheek. It wasn't sexual in nature, more thankful.

"What was that for?"

"You *like* me," she sang, teasingly as she batted her eyes. "You want to kiss me."

Tristan laughed. He liked this side of Karon. The flirty, girly part that she didn't show to just anyone. It was a blessing to be on the receiving end of one of her teasing grins, and Tristan had made it a point to bring it out as often as he could. "I want more than a kiss."

"I don't know." Sitting prim and proper, Karon folded her hands together demurely on her lap and crossed her legs at the ankle. "I'm a good girl, and good girls don't put out."

Number seven, Tristan reminded himself with a smile—role-playing. Delivering a move Fonzie would have been proud of, Tristan faked a yawn, stretching his arms high in the air before dropping his right one over the headrest so he could rest his hand on her shoulder. "But I'm the captain of the football team. I have a reputation to protect."

"As class treasurer and president of the debate club, I too have a reputation to protect."

Smiling, Tristan twirled her hair around his finger, loving the way the full curl wrapped its way around his fingertips, much like the owner was beginning to wrap her hands around his heart. "Is that the way you see yourself, debate club president?"

"It's what I was."

"But this isn't your high school. This is our high school. You can be anyone you want to be."

"A Brazen Badass." Karon's voice took on a dreamlike quality. "I can be the bad girl who put out, the one all the boys liked."

"And all the girls hated." Tristan remembered those little harlots fondly. They had the skills to turn a boy into a man with a simple twist of their hips. He owed his own misplaced virginity to one Tammy Mae Jents. Good Lord, it was a sin for a sixteen-year-old girl to be that skilled. "I liked those girls."

"I hated them." Karon smiled, lost in her own memories. "Especially because she got to go out with the captain of the football team."

"Then it's definitely time for a little role reversal, Karon. Be bad. Be as bad as you want to be."

"As bad as I want?"

"As bad as you dare."

The teasing look in her eyes told Tristan more than her words ever could how much she was enjoying the little impromptu role-playing. He was willing to bet that in high school, Karon could have had her pick of the boys, but she hadn't then nor did she now understand her appeal to the opposite sex.

To Tristan, it was as obvious as water is wet. Karon was everything any man would want. The longer he was around her, the more he liked her, and not just because they were going through more rubbers than the Indy 500. He truly liked her.

Tristan could, and literally had, talked to her for hours about everything and nothing at all. Karon was smart, sexy as all get out and she made a man feel like a man. It had been a long time since Tristan had felt that way about a woman.

"So, what do bad girls like you do with boys in parked cars?"

"Anything they want."

Tristan liked the sound of that. Leaning over the console again, Karon brushed her lips across Tristan's neck as she slid her hand teasingly against his chest.

"Do you want to get in the backseat?" he asked, trying to recall if that line had ever worked for him in high school.

"What can we do back there that we can't do up here?"

"A lot."

"No." Running her hand down his chest to the buckle of his pants, Karon caressed the outline his hard cock was making. Christ, they hadn't even done anything and he was as hard as steel. "I think we should stay right where we are."

Tristan gripped her hand in his, pressing it down firmly on his crotch, just in case she didn't get the hint. "You might want to reconsider."

"Why is that?"

"Because it's going to be awfully hard to fuck you in this seat."

"I'd say it's hard." Giving him a teasing look, Karon squeezed his cock firmly. "But we don't have to get into the backseat to have fun."

Karon wiggled her hand under his until Tristan released his hold on her. When her hand was free, Karon began to unbuckle his belt, all the while maintaining eye contact. She had freed his cock from the confines of his pants as Tristan watched silently, wondering what his little vixen was up to.

"There's a lot more room in the back," he tried again, biting back a groan when she began to slide her hand leisurely up and down his rigid shaft.

"Just because you're the most popular boy at our school doesn't mean I'm going to let you have your way with me."

"I thought you were the bad girl."

"I changed my mind. I think good girls have more fun. I know I'm having a great time now."

"I'm having a better one."

Karon's husky chuckle sent a surge through his already aching cock. Tristan never would have thought that a simple hand job could feel so good. The roles had quickly reversed and he was the one holding on for dear life for control as she teased him unmercifully.

Hell, it was like high school all over again. The evening was becoming a bit too nostalgic for him now.

"Come on, Karon, let's get in the back. I want to feel more than your hand surrounding me. I want you."

"You've got me."

"Fine, I want your hot, sweet pussy."

"What will you give me if I go back there with you?"

Nine inches didn't seem like the thing to say, although it was exactly what Tristan was thinking. "Pleasure."

"You're not enjoying this?"

"I'm enjoying it immensely. But not as much as I would enjoy fucking you."

Bringing her hand once more to the tip of his cock, Karon ran her fingers around his slick head before bringing them to her mouth to taste. "I'll race you to the back, the last one there is on the bottom."

Chuckling as Karon quickly opened her door and got out, Tristan tried to stuff his arousal back in his pants. "No fair," he called over his shoulder when Karon dove into the backseat. "You had an unfair advantage."

"How's this for an advantage?" Karon leaned over and nipped his ear, dropping a silk scrap of material in his lap.

Yelping at the sting of pain, Tristan pulled away, amused by her girlish behavior. Karon was coming out of the sheltered shell she'd formed around herself and Tristan was happy he was along for the ride.

As he opened the car door, the car light came on, shining brightly on the red slip of silk in his lap. Picking it up, Tristan chuckled when he realized they were her panties. He glanced over his shoulder at Karon, who was looking demure and smug all at the same time. "Did you forget something?"

"No, those are yours. I thought all boys wanted a trophy of their conquests."

"So true." Tristan leaned forward and draped the panties over his rearview mirror, showing off his prize of the night.

"Tristan," Karon gasped, her eyes alight with humor. "You can't leave them there."

"Yes I can. All of us bragging boys do." Slipping out of the car, Tristan quickly closed the driver door as he opened the backseat passenger door, trying to disappear into the car without being extremely obvious.

The plan of course didn't work. As he leaned out to close the door, horns honked, lights flashed and voices rang out their approval. Tristan chuckled. Some things never really changed.

"Was all of that for us?"

"Yes, we now have everyone's attention. They'll be waiting for the windows to fog up and for the back of the car to begin its mating dance."

Scooting over to him, Karon climbed on him and straddled his lap. "Let's give them something to honk at."

"Baby, you took the words right out of my mouth." Reaching between them, Tristan quickly unbuttoned his pants, bringing his still-aroused member out to the party.

The peasant skirt Karon wore was perfect for easy-access fucking. Slipping his hands under the long, loose skirt, Tristan ran his palms against her soft thighs to the heart of her damp, downy curls. Apparently, Tristan wasn't the only person the hand job was working for.

"What's this?" he teased, brushing his fingers through her dampness, seeking her clit. "If I didn't know better, I'd think you *liked* me."

"I do."

"And you like the things I do to you." Tristan ran his finger in circles around her erect little bud, enjoying the sound of Karon's moans. "All the dirty little games we play. All the naughty little things you love."

"Yes, I like them all." She moaned, pushing her pussy down

onto his seeking fingers, but as she arched toward him, Tristan drew his hand away. "Tristan, please don't tease me."

"Like you teased me earlier?" he asked, reaching behind him on the window sill to grab the condoms he had stashed there earlier. Quickly sheathing his erection, Tristan grabbed his cock in his hand and brought it up to the slick opening of Karon's pussy. "I guess bad girls like you are used to being in charge, but let me tell you something, princess. I'm in charge back here."

"Fine, you're in charge." Karon moved down until her legs encased his hips, positioning herself to sink onto his cock. But Tristan had other plans.

"Not yet, Karon." Tristan refused to fuck her without tasting her melons first. He loved her breasts. Breasts in general, really, but Karon's breasts were built for him. "Give me what I want."

Without having to ask, Karon lifted the ends of her shirt over her breasts and freed the heavy twins to his impatient hands.

"Feed them to me. Offer them to me," Tristan demanded, ignoring the ache in his groin. His cock and his hunger weren't on the same accord, but they both would be appeased before the night was over.

"Taste me," she begged, although the offer wasn't necessary. Tristan was already laving her nipples before the words were past her lips. His mouth moved from one hard nipple to the other, milking the hard peaks as he bathed them with his tongue.

Karon's fingers replaced his between the core of her thighs. She fingered herself as he lost himself in her breasts. "Fuck me, Tristan, please."

"No, Karon, fuck me." Jerking her to him, Tristan released her breasts as Karon pushed down onto his waiting cock.

Their voices echoed in passion as Karon's body engulfed his cock. It felt like an eternity since he had last been inside her welcoming depths. Her heat was destined to burn him whole as she rose up, nearly unseating herself, before humping down again.

Even with him slouched down in the seat, there was still little room to maneuver the way that he wanted. But they managed to find a rhythm and motion that soon had the windows fogged and the rear axles bumping.

No longer caring if the world at large was watching, Tristan instead concentrated on the way she felt around him. Karon was so damn tight, even with how wet she was, it seemed to take an act of God to slide in all the way. She fit him to a tee, her body made for him and for him alone.

"Play with your nipples," Tristan ordered. If he wasn't touching them, he wanted her to be. Her breasts were objects of beauty and they deserved to be worshipped.

Karon complied with his orders—cupping her breasts, she gripped the berry tips, squeezing them, teasing them, for both of their pleasures.

The light from the screen penetrated the fog-covered windows, illuminating their passionate embrace, casting an erotic glow onto Karon's enraptured body. She looked like a goddess. Her pale body, bathed in the celluloid radiance from the screen was as erotic as the little guttural sounds she was making while she rode him. Tristan's own angel of mercy coming forth to carry him to paradise.

Tristan dug his nails into her thighs, gripping her tighter as she picked up her speed. The choppy moans Karon was making in the back of her throat signaled her oncoming orgasm. It was a sign that Tristan had learned very well in the last weeks. One that he looked forward to hearing as much as possible.

"Yes . . . yes . . . Tris . . . fuck me . . . more," she cried, her ragged plea echoing throughout the small confines of the car.

"You want more? I'll give you more." Slipping his hand between them, Tristan grasped her clit between his fingers and milked it for all it was worth, dragging her orgasm from her rung by rung.

Karon screamed as she came, grinding her pelvis down onto him, bucking in his arms as she cried his name. The sound of his name on her lips triggered Tristan's own release. He fucked up into her with hard, deep thrusts that dragged whimpers from Karon's shivering body.

"So good, baby, so good." Humping up, he rode out the wave, throwing his head back as he came, her name a whisper on his dry lips and a roar in his head.

The air around them seemed to chill in record time. Tristan wasn't sure if it was because the window was partially down, housing the speaker box, or because of the sweat dampening their overworked bodies. All he knew was loving had never been that good before with any other woman. Nor would he have gone to such lengths to please another woman. But pleasing Karon was different. She was his.

Karon lay against him, her skin as damp as the stuffy air within the car. The loud applause from outside the car startled her into sitting up. The crowd around them was going crazy. Cars were honking, lights were flashing and engines were revving. To judge from the sounds generating from the speaker box, the movie was over, which surprised the hell out of Tristan. How long had they been going at it anyway?

With a soft sigh, Karon eased up off him and sat down next to him, leaning her head against his shoulder once more. "Do you think the applause was for us or for the movie?"

Unable to help himself, Tristan burst out laughing, pulling her tighter into him. "If it wasn't for us, it damn sure should have been."

SIX

*T*HERE WAS JUST SOMETHING about being made love to all night long that put a little extra jaunt in Karon's step. Continuous sexual bliss was something she could seriously get used to. And waking up in Tristan's arms was a perk she could handle as well.

The man had stamina that would put a seventeen-year-old boy to shame and Karon was loving every second, or should she say inch, of it. Not that it was just about the sex. The sex was great, but just being with Tristan was wonderful.

He was immensely funny, kind to a fault and, in general, a really good man. If it weren't for the lack of permanency in their relationship, Karon would be completely happy. It was a really odd feeling—the desire for permanency—for Karon because she had been running from real relationships all her life. Always putting something before it. School, friends, work, everything was a substitute for the real thing.

Even her on-again, off-again relationship with Walter couldn't be classified as a *real* relationship. Not that he had hinted at wanting anything deeper. Walter had seemed as content as she thought she was. *Thought* being the key word, seeing as how she was more than content with Tristan.

And Karon was going to do everything in her power to keep it that way. Tristan seemed to want things light with no commitments and Karon was fine with that. It was what she wanted too, kind of. Maybe light with a hint of permanent on the side.

She was officially a Brazen Badass. She had a killer career, a man who made her weak in the knees and finally, for the first time in her entire life, a wonderful sex life. Life just couldn't get any better.

"Karon, Mr. Bonner is here to see you."

Damn, Walter! She'd spoken too soon.

"He doesn't have an appointment but—"

Karon hit the intercom button, cutting Gail, her secretary, off. "It's okay. Send him in."

Standing up, Karon smoothed down the creases in her skirt and walked around her desk with a smile etched into her face. She and Walter may not be dating anymore, but she did still consider him a friend . . . of sorts.

"Karon." Walter boomed her name, as if she were across the street instead of right in front of him. It was one of the many things about the husky man that drove Karon crazy, but also endeared him to her.

Small in height but not in personality, Walter was affable if nothing else. His cheery outlook made it hard to stay mad at him for any given length of time, giving way to the main reason they tended to get back together so often. His cherub face filled with happiness as he walked over to Karon, arms extended wide.

"Hello, Walter." Karon clasped him in a quick hug before doling out the expected kiss. "How have you been?"

"Great, but when haven't I?" he cheerfully replied, before sitting himself down on the love seat. "So sit. Talk to me. Bring me up to date on your world."

"You have a few hours?"

"For you, I have all the time in the world." Unbuttoning his gray suit jacket, Walter made himself comfortable on the sofa. His stout frame took up most of the love seat but he scooted over to make room for her.

Walter wasn't a heavyset man, just a bulky one, but with his jolly persona, Jacque had always likened him to Santa, an image Karon always thought of when they were together.

Sitting down next him, Karon began to fill him in on what he'd missed out on in the last two months. Walter owned his own computer consulting business and traveled often, but every time he came back to town he made it a point to stop in to see her, even if they weren't seeing each other at the time. They chatted for what seemed like only minutes but in fact was nearly an hour, and before Karon knew it, Gail was buzzing her again.

"Your lunch date is here, Karon."

Lunch date. That only meant one thing. Tristan. Unaware she was smiling, Karon stood up quickly and moved to open the door.

"So you're seeing someone new."

The surprise in Walter's voice was as shocking as the wounded look on his face. Karon quickly lowered her hand from the door and turned back to him. "Yes, I am."

"Good guy?"

"I think so."

"That's great." Standing up, he smiled, although it didn't reach his gray eyes. "You deserve a good guy."

Despite everything bad she'd ever said about him, Walter was a nice guy. A good guy even, he just wasn't the one for her. Nor was she the one for him.

"I've been blessed with a couple of those."

Walter chuckled as she had intended. Walking to her, Walter pulled her in for a hug. Karon lingered there for a moment, instinctively knowing this was probably going to be one of the last times she was this close to him. Five years was a long time to be with someone, even if it wasn't true love.

"Am I interrupting?"

Pulling back, Karon turned around and faced a frowning Tristan, who was standing in the doorway. The sight of him alone took her breath away. It didn't matter how many times she'd seen him or how long she was around him, Karon simply couldn't get enough of him.

"No, I was just leaving." Walter released his hold on Karon, pulling her from her lustful thoughts of Tristan. Even in another man's arms, she fantasized about him. She was so gone. "Don't be a stranger."

"You either." She smiled. Unable to resist, she brushed another kiss against his cheek, this time doing it to egg on Tristan.

Karon wasn't the type to try to make a man jealous, but Tristan's accusing tone amused her. As if she'd really have a tryst in the middle of the day with her ex-boyfriend. Hell, she didn't have the energy.

Walter nodded to Tristan as he walked past him, which only

made Tristan scowl more. As soon as Walter exited the room, Tristan shut the door and locked it before turning back around. "Was that who I thought it was?"

"It depends." Karon bit back a smile as she walked to her desk. She needed time to compose her expression before she faced him again or she'd just break out in laughter. His caveman tone was so not like him, which made it all the more enjoyable.

"On?"

"On who you think it is. I'm not a mind reader, you know."

"I know you're heading the right way for a sore behind."

"Hmm . . . " Karon fought hard to keep her smile at bay. Tristan was downright adorable when he was irked. "Anal sex again? I thought we already marked it off *the* list."

"Karon . . . " he growled, taking a menacing step toward her.

"Tristan . . . " Responding in the same tone, Karon placed her hands on her hips. Men! Big babies all of them, and hers was the cutest of them all.

"Why was Walter here to see you?"

"To visit."

"Because . . . ?"

"Because he was on this side of town." Karon walked over to Tristan, who was scowling like a well-dressed, perturbed seven-year-old, and patted his cheek mockingly. "You know you don't have to be jealous of him."

Tristan snorted. "Jealous of him. I don't think so."

"Good." *He was so jealous.*

"I mean, this is a man who couldn't make you come in five years."

"I never said that I didn't have orgasms with Walter." Karon moved past Tristan and went to unlock the door when he walked up behind her and held it closed with his palm flat against it.

"Yes. You did."

Turning until her back was against the wall, Karon smiled up at him, bemused. "No. I said that he didn't like oral sex or a lot of variety. Other than that, Walter was fine in bed."

"Other than that."

"Yes, other than that. You know sex isn't everything. I'm sure with all the little tricks and skills I've picked up from you in the last few weeks or so, I could teach Walter a few things."

"I don't think so." Tristan stepped even closer, nearly a breath away from Karon. She felt pinned, and for some odd reason she liked it. The fierce scowl, the biting words, the menacing pose worked for her.

"Possessive, aren't we?"

"Are you trying to make me jealous, Karon?"

"Can I?" The thought of Tristan being aggravated over Walter suited her perverse humor. As if Tristan ever had to worry about being in competition with him.

"You try my patience, woman." Tristan's smile seemed a bit strained.

"And you were jealous. Admit it."

"No."

Laughing, Karon circled her arms around his waist and pulled him to her. She didn't need the words. Karon knew the truth. "Give me a kiss."

"I'm about to give you a spanking."

"That works too."

Tristan's words sent shivers down her body. That was one fantasy they hadn't done yet, but she was definitely up for it. Apparently, she wasn't the only one. Tristan began to harden against her, much to her delight, and the feel of his arousal started a chain reaction in her own.

Karon's nipples rose to rigid peaks under her bra, the lace scratching the sensitive tips. Wetting her dry lips, Karon stared into Tristan's eyes, seeing the lust she felt echoed back in his big brown eyes.

Would she ever get her fill of him?

Tilting her head back, she kissed Tristan gently on the lips, a mere brush of skin to skin before pulling back. The brief contact did little to appease the desire growing inside her, only whetting her appetite for him.

Tristan looked down at her with a soft smile. The irritated look was gone from his eyes. In its place, simmering arousal. "Is that all I get?"

Karon had to clear her throat twice before she answered him. "In my office during business hours, yes."

Nudging the side of her neck with his lips, Tristan turned the tables on Karon, teasing her with his body, as she had done with her words. "I recall sex at work being on your list."

"A mistake, I assure you." Karon could feel her pussy pulsating with need. The very thought of Tristan taking her on her desk did things to her that making love with other men never had.

She wanted him. Here and now, but Karon knew better. They would never get away with it. Once Tristan was inside of her, she would be loud and demanding and they would have an audience in seconds.

"Chicken," he whispered against her neck.

"Damn straight."

Laughing, Tristan pulled back. "Then let's get out of here before it's too late."

Looking at him, smiling and carefree, Karon knew it was already too late. She was in love.

IT WAS A SIMPLE PLAN REALLY. Barbecue a few steaks, uncover the pool and sauna so they could enjoy the last rays of smog-filled sunshine and just relax. A foolproof plan if ever there was one. There was only one problem Tristan hadn't figured on—Karon in a swimsuit.

Today was supposed to be about her. Tristan had intended to pamper her, romance her and then have his wicked way with her, in that order. But after seeing her in that slick, green one-piece, all he could think of was slipping the emerald straps off her shoulders and burying his cock between her lush breasts.

He was lucky she hadn't changed into her suit until after dinner or the steaks never would have been cooked.

Easing down into the water, Karon hissed at the heat. Tristan let out his own little hiss as her beautiful breasts disappeared under a mound of bubbles. After two months of continuous sexual exploration, Tristan would have thought he was over the hard-at-a-glance stage. Yet here he was, aroused at the mere hint of cleavage bobbing up and down in the water. He was a sick, sick man.

Hell, he didn't even know why she bothered wearing a suit. He was going have her out of it in a few seconds anyway.

Karon sighed orgasmically as she leaned back in the Jacuzzi, making Tristan smile. She looked like a marooned mermaid with her auburn hair floating around like waves. She was beautiful, and Tristan was willing to bet she didn't think so. The truly beautiful ones never did.

Setting her glass of wine next to her on the ledge, Tristan unbuckled his pants and dropped them along with his boxers to the ground. Karon's eyes lit up as she watched him step into the spa, causing him to chuckle at her wide-eyed stare.

Tristan felt like his cock grew ten inches under her wanton stare. *Damn, she was good for his ego.*

"Thanks for dinner."

"It was my pleasure."

Smiling at him, Karon took a sip out of her wineglass before setting it back down on the sideboard. She looked utterly relaxed and at peace, the only thing that was going according to his plan. "I've never had a guy cook for me."

For some reason Tristan wasn't surprised. From what he could tell, Karon had missed out on a lot of things she shouldn't have. The main one being treated decently by someone. "Well, you can cross it off your list."

"It wasn't on *the* list." She laughed, still refusing to call it her list. It had become a private joke between them, one that Tristan loved to tease her with.

"It should have been right between anal sex, airplanes and"— gesturing to their liquid surroundings, Tristan added—"sex in the water."

"We did that already. Remember the shower?"

"I recall I made a rule that we do each number as many times as I like."

"Let it never be said that I don't like to follow rules." Karon was fast becoming a little temptress right before his eyes. No one in his right mind would call her a Goody Two-shoes again.

Pulling her toward him, Tristan had her straddling his lap as he bent forward to kiss her. She tasted sweet like the berry wine, her lips and tongue coated with its sugary essence. The liquor was just as intoxicating radiating off her as it had been in the vat.

Karon moaned into his mouth as she gyrated gently down on his cock. Just a thin layer of material separated them and yet it felt like the Great Wall of China. Tristan drew her tongue into his mouth while slipping her bathing-suit straps down from her shoulders. He wanted her bare and riding him, not dry-humping like a pair of horny teenagers.

Breaking away from the kiss, Tristan concentrated on pulling the wet suit down her torso, groaning when her breasts broke free from their constraints. Karon's rouge-tinted nipples peeked from the bubbling water, making Tristan hunger for the tips.

"Now for dessert." Cupping his hand under her bottom, Tristan brought Karon up out of the water a bit, until her breasts were level with his face.

Breasts. The next best thing to pussy. Pulling her to him, Tristan covered a nipple with his mouth, laving her tightened tip with his tongue. Maybe he hadn't been breastfed enough as a child because Tristan had a serious nipple fetish. He could bathe the twin peaks all day long and never get tired. And to judge from the moans coming from Karon, she would let him.

After making sure he paid equal attention to the delicious twins, Tristan pulled back, his breathing just as harsh as Karon's.

"Stand up and step out of this," he ordered harshly, impatient to have the beauty ride him.

Looking around nervously, Karon did as he bid. "Someone might see."

"No one can see. The property's fenced all around." To be honest, Tristan could care less right now. The only thing he was concerned with was getting inside her. "Besides, just think, we're knocking out number sixteen."

Turning Karon until her back faced him, Tristan eased his cock between her slick folds, slowly lowering her down onto his length. He gasped as her heat swallowed him, loving the feeling of her sweet body engulfing him. "Ride me, baby," he ordered, pushing up into her, sinking his teeth down into her shoulder.

Palming her heavy mounds, Tristan squeezed her taut nipples between his fingers, milking a response from her parted lips as she fucked him. Water splashed around them as they rocked into each other like waves crashing into the sand.

Between the heat generating from the spa and the heat radiating between them, Tristan was surprised they just didn't combust. Grasping her bouncing hips in his hands, Tristan slowed down her jaunt, intent on making it lasting and memorable. "Hold on, baby."

Karon dug her fingernails in his arms, gripping Tristan as he made his way across to the other side. Leaning his knees against the bench, Tristan angled Karon until her feet were flat on the bench and her legs were spread wide.

"What are you doing?" she panted, reaching out to grasp the wall.

"Just sit back and enjoy."

Tristan slid his hand down to her mound, spreading her lips with his probing fingers. Pulling back, he slipped his cock out of her cunt, bracing his legs more firmly apart. Tristan shifted them until he felt the rush of the jets against his hands and smiled to himself. *This mermaid was in for a hell of a ride.*

Tristan knew the second Karon felt the rushing water shooting directly on her clit, because her back bowed and she let out the sweetest moan ever heard by man. Dropping her head back on his shoulder, Karon held on for dear life to Tristan's hand, undulating her hips toward the stream.

"Oh, oh, oh," she moaned, trembling in his arms as the jets stimulated her clit.

Tristan wanted to work his cock back inside of her, but he knew he wouldn't be able to fuck her and keep the jet centered on her clit so he just held back, letting Karon enjoy her ride. From the look of her arching body, it was a hell of a ride.

"That's it, mermaid, come for me." Tristan was more turned on than he could ever remember being.

With her back bowed, Tristan looked down into her passion-filled face. Eyes closed as if lost in ecstasy, Karon had never looked more beautiful to him. Her lips were parted as if in silent prayer, muttering words too low for him to hear. It was almost as if she were speaking another language, absent from all reality except for what was taking place there in the water.

Her release came faster than he'd expected, raining down heavily upon her. Rearing up in his arms, Karon cried out, "Tristan . . . yes . . . oh . . ."

Unable to resist any longer, Tristan quickly stood, spinning Karon around until she was once again facing him. Sitting her on the edge of the spa, he parted her legs and slid into her welcoming depth.

"God," he groaned, finally where he belonged, balls-deep in his woman.

Half in the water and half out, Tristan gripped her cheeks in his hand, using them as a lever for their sexual romp. Wrapping her legs around him, Karon cradled him to her as he pumped into her with the image of her coming still blazing in his head.

Karon's body was held up by her arms, bent to angle her for a deeper thrust. And thrust deep he did. His body rocked into hers as the water splashed around them, echoing their chaotic sexual dance.

The deeper he went, the tighter she gripped him with her legs. Both ground into each other until Karon screamed out his name, dragging Tristan over the edge with her.

It took everything out of him to remember to pull out. But he did, just in time to see his semen spill into his gripping fist. Falling forward, Tristan caught himself with one hand as he continued to pump his cock.

"Fuck," he muttered, caught up in the passion of the night. Shivering, he shook as the last tremors pulsated through his body.

"Oh my Gawd." Karon's leg had fallen back into the water and she looked as out of breath as he felt.

"You can say that again."

"Why the hell wasn't that on my list?"

The sincerity in her voice caused Tristan to laugh as he eased back up. Grabbing a towel off the deck, he wiped his hand and himself clean before handing it to her. "You gotta love the jets."

"I'd say." Sinking back into the water, Karon looked as if she was ready to pass out. "Now I know why people own Jacuzzis. You would think a perk like that would be highlighted on the box."

"It is," Tristan teased, getting out of the water. "It's just in small print."

"I've got to get one of these."

"No need. You can just come hump my jets any time you want."

Karon reached over and grabbed the towel he had dropped, balled it up and threw it at him. "Brat."

Tristan easily dodged the towel, catching it in midair, much to Karon's disgust. Tossing it on a deck chair, Tristan dressed in his jeans again before grabbing his beer off the table.

Life was great. Looking over at Karon, Tristan felt his heart kick up an extra beat. She was so goddamn beautiful. His own personal mermaid. Life just didn't get much better than this.

"Don't fall asleep in there," he warned as he sat on a lounge chair. Tristan wanted to take a few minutes to enjoy the evening air before he moved her back into the house and took sweet advantage of her.

"I won't. I'm just thinking."

"About what?"

"My friends. You know they think I'm crazy."

"Really?"

"Not all of them, just Zoya. She thinks this going to end badly."

"And you said?" Tristan asked casually.

"Not much. Jacque did most of the talking for me." She

laughed, taking a sip of her wine. "She's much more experienced in matters like these and Zoya is a bit jaded. She tends to—"

"Matters like these?"

Karon gestured between the two of them. "You know, casual relationships."

The fact that the word *relationship* didn't send up a red flag should have been a first sign that something was up, and instead of being freaked at the way this conversation was going, Tristan was becoming irritated. *Casual relationship.* Is that what she thought they had, a *casual relationship*?

"No, I don't know, Karon. Why don't you explain it a bit more to me? What exactly is a casual relationship?"

Startled, Karon looked up at him, confusion marring her brow. "Umm, a relationship that is casual. You know, not formal or anything."

"By not formal you mean not exclusive?" Tristan's words came out sharp.

"I guess. Why are you upset?" Setting her glass down on the deck, Karon moved out of the water until she was sitting on the edge next to Tristan's lounge chair. "I just thought you'd be amused."

"Yeah, amused." Standing up, Tristan moved down from the spa, needing some room to think. "So does this mean you're seeing other men?"

The words were out before he could stop them. Jealousy rose up hard and quick inside of him at the thought of Karon with anyone else.

"What other men? There's only been you and Walter for the last five years. Remember, I'm the woman going through the drought."

Five years was a long time to be with someone, especially if the sex was bad. "Five years is a long time to be with someone to have it not end up with marriage."

"Not everyone wants to get married," she replied with a shrug.

That was true. Tristan himself was knocking on forty and hadn't been married, but he also hadn't been in a relationship with anyone that was half a decade long. "Do you?"

For some reason the thought of marriage and Karon just seemed to work for him. He could imagine a bunch of overorganized kids running around making lists and color-coding their toys.

"I want to get married someday, but I didn't want to marry Walter."

"Why?"

"Because we just didn't seem like forever to me."

"But you stayed with him for five years. Did you consider that casual too?"

Frowning, Karon stood. The breeze ruffled around her long hair as she battled to wrap the tropical towel around her body. "I never cheated on him, if that's your question."

"Because you guys didn't have a 'casual relationship'?" Those two words were still rubbing him raw.

"No, because I'm not that kind of person." Stepping in front of him, Karon faced him, frowning. "What's the problem, Tristan? I thought we both wanted the same thing."

"Which was?"

"To have fun."

Fun. So that's all he was to her. Someone to help check off

a list. "I think we can both agree we've had enough fun for one night."

"Oh yeah, I think we left funville a while back." Brushing past him, Karon stormed into his house, slamming the door after her.

"Son of a bitch," Tristan roared, throwing the can across the lawn. What kind of fucked-up shit was this? Tristan had to force himself not to follow Karon into the house, because the way he was feeling right now, they'd be crossing spanking off of her list of *might do* real quick.

If Karon thought she was just going to fuck him and then leave him, she'd better think again. This wasn't a list thing, it was a forever thing.

SEVEN

"SO LET ME GET THIS STRAIGHT." Jacque's long-suffering sigh was grating on Karon's nerves. The last thing she wanted to deal with was Jacque's dramatics—she just wanted to understand what went wrong yesterday. "You basically called him a human vibrator and you can't understand why he would be upset?"

"I did not call him a human vibrator." Karon put as much rage as she could behind her whispered words. How dare Jacque take his side? She was supposed to be on Karon's.

"Girl, please, you damn near called him a whore."

"Whose side are you on?" she bellowed, cringing when the couple walking past her door shot her a questioning glare. This impromptu phone call was going to have clients fleeing in moral outrage. She should have known better than to call Jacque when she was at work. Gesturing for Gail, who was trying to appear as though she wasn't eavesdropping, to shut her door, Karon tried to calm down. This was not how she had expected this phone call to go. "Excuse me, what number did I call? I could have sworn this was Jacque's number and not Zoya's."

"For once Zoya and I would be in agreement. You don't treat your boy toy like that. He's got feelings too, you know."

"I know he has feelings, I just didn't know he might have feelings for me."

"Why not? You have feelings for him."

The truth of Jacque's words silenced her as nothing else could. Was it so obvious to everyone but Tristan how she felt for him?

"Did you think he was just in it for the sex?"

"Well . . . yes." Or she did before she saw the way her words affected him.

"Girl, you didn't place the ad. Tristan isn't a stud, trying to pay his rent. He's a man, and heaven help me for saying this, and it looks like a good one."

Sighing, Karon sat back in her chair. She didn't need Jacque to tell her that Tristan was a good man. She'd known that from the start. Karon was just trying to follow the rules she thought every Brazen Badass did. That was the way she thought he wanted her to act. No pressures, no worries, just sex.

That's what she got for thinking.

"So what should I do?"

"Do I need to make you a list?"

"Good God, no. No more lists. Lists are what got me in trouble in the first damn place."

"No, being uncouth got you in trouble, but that's okay. Mama Jacque is here to save your fine ass."

Karon couldn't resist rolling her eyes. "If I recall, it was Mama Jacque's bad advice that got me in the situation in the first place. Maybe if I would have been more myself, none of this would have ever happened."

"Damn straight it wouldn't." The annoyance in Jacque's voice wasn't hard to detect. "You wouldn't have made a list. You wouldn't have turned your friendship into moreship and you would have still been unhappy. Go right ahead and blame me."

"Jacque . . ."

"No, friendship . . . terminated." With those parting words, Jacque hung up the phone.

"Drama queen," Karon muttered under her breath, leaning forward to dial her friend's number again. Whenever one of them disagreed with or annoyed the other, the friendship would be terminated, meaning of course that the annoyer or disagreer had to call back to soothe the wounded ego. Thousands of years of evolution and it resorted to this. "Friendship is not terminated."

"It's going to be . . . some day."

Snorting, Karon seriously doubted that. They all loved each other way too much for that to happen. "Okay, you know what we need?"

"A man with a tongue like Gene Simmons's and a body like Tyson Beckford's."

"Amen, sister." She couldn't argue with that. "But besides that?"

"A fat-free, calorie-free, full-flavored crème brûlée to be invented and for cellulite to be considered the new 'in' thing."

"Shut up." Karon laughed, beginning to feel better already.

"Then don't ask me what we need. Tell me."

"Fine, we need a girls' night out."

"Are we talking fuck-me pumps, push-up bras and margaritas?"

"Oh yes." It was just what the doctor ordered.

"Oh yeah, my calves and back are hurting already."

"So Kutcher's at seven."

"I'll call Zoya."

Her girls, margaritas and loud music, everything was going to be okay. "Hey, Jacque."

"Yes."

"I love you."

"Of course you do."

GOD SHE HATED JACQUE, and Zoya was on her shit list. Girls' night out was an official thing of the past.

She was getting too old to be dealing with hangovers. Walking as slowly as she could, Karon made her way to her front door, praying that whoever was leaning on the doorbell would just die.

The doorbell had been ringing for what felt like an hour and in her silly, inebriated state, Karon had just assumed that the person would get the hint when she didn't answer the door after the first ten thousand dings and go away.

She was wrong. Very wrong.

Grasping for the handle, Karon had to fight her robe to find her hand. The damn thing weighed a ton and was trying to suffocate her. When she finally freed herself from her terry-cloth fetter, she attacked the handle, fighting to open the door for several seconds before she remembered to unlock it.

Opening the door was proving to be a far greater challenge than she was really willing to face this early in the afternoon. And the damn bell wouldn't stop ringing.

"I'm coming, damn it."

"Karon, is that you?"

Tristan? Twisting the handle with all her might, Karon finally opened the door, unleashing a floodgate of bright sunshine. "Oh Gawd," she muttered, shielding her face from the deadly glare.

"Karon, what happened?"

Gesturing for him to come in, Karon stepped back, almost falling on the defeated robe, lying like a puddle in her entryway. "Come in but don't yell."

"I didn't yell." Pushing her back into the house, Tristan shut the door behind him with a resounding bang. "Where does it hurt?"

Where didn't it hurt was a better question. "I'm okay."

"Damn it, you're not okay. Did someone hurt you?"

"Yes, Senorita Margarita. I need coffee and lots of it." Heading toward the kitchen, Karon didn't bother to see if Tristan followed. She was having a hard enough time getting there herself.

Pulling on the freezer door was as big a chore as opening the front door. Karon was about to give up and just lick her coffeepot when Tristan stepped behind her, placing his hands over hers, and pulled open the door.

"Why don't you let me do this?"

Karon didn't even mind the humor in his voice. As long as Tristan made coffee, he could laugh quietly at her all day.

"God bless you." Walking to the island, she pulled out a stool and sat down, burying her face in her arms.

Tristan worked in silence and soon the smell of perking coffee began to fill the room. Karon was so lost in her own personal hell that she didn't even notice Tristan had moved behind her until he began to massage her scalp, instantly sending waves of relief coursing through her aching temple.

"Was it a birthday party?" His voice was low and his hands were firm, working together to soothe her.

"No, it was a 'Karon is an idiot' party."

His hands paused for a second. "And I wasn't invited?"

Karon smiled at his tone, easing up into a sitting position. When the room didn't spin, she let out a sigh of relief.

"Let me get your coffee for you."

"I can do it." It was the least she could do. Besides, it felt wrong for Tristan to be so nice to her when they were fighting because of her.

"I know you can, Karon, but I want to." Walking to the pot, Tristan poured her a cup, making himself at home in her kitchen. It felt right. More right than any other man had.

Setting the cup in front of her, Tristan turned and made himself one. "Are you nauseous?"

"No." Thank God. Karon didn't think she could handle the noise throwing up would make. "I just have a drum parade having a fiesta in my head. José is a killer."

"Yes he is."

Karon's first sip of coffee was almost orgasmic. The warm heat instantly spread throughout her body, sending shots of caffeine to the restrained blood vessels in her head. She might live after all.

Looking up, Karon caught Tristan smiling down at her. For the first time since she opened the door, she thought about how she must look to him. As usual, he was dressed nice. Casual slacks and a pullover shirt did nothing but emphasize his nice physique. He was smooth-shaven and looked as if he'd stepped off the pages of GQ magazine, where she, on the other hand, probably looked like Chewbacca's love child.

Karon picked her spoon off the island and peered at herself. Chewbacca wouldn't even claim her. Her fiery red hair stood on end and she had bags big enough to pack for a safari vacation. So not the image she had wanted to present to Tristan the next time she saw him.

"If you had any kindness in you at all, you'd kill me," she said, half jokingly.

"Now why would I want to do that?"

"Because I look like who done it and why."

"I think you look beautiful. It's nice to see you ruffled for a change."

Snorting, she tipped her cup to him. "Wish granted."

Returning the gesture, Tristan smiled. "I'd say. What were you guys thinking last night?"

"We weren't, that was the problem. You know, this is all your fault."

"My fault?"

"Yep. It all started out with me boohooing to Jacque about you being mean to me."

"I was being mean?"

So it wasn't the exact truth, but it wasn't like Karon was going to admit that she was in the wrong. "Hey, it's my story and I'm sticking to it."

Snorting, Tristan pulled out a seat and sat down. "Please continue."

"Thank you. That somehow led to her suggesting drinks and

fuck-me pumps and the next thing I know, you're banging on my door like a man possessed."

"Fuck-me pumps?"

"Don't ask." The pain began to ease behind her tired eyes. Stretching her arms, Karon caught a whiff of her underarms and quickly lowered them. "I need to go shower."

"How about you finish your coffee and I get it started for you?"

That was it. Starting the shower was where Karon drew the line. "What's going on? You're being far too nice."

"Don't you deserve it?" His tone seemed a bit mocking but Karon couldn't be sure. It was either attitude or the last shot.

"No." Not according to Jacque, Zoya and her conscience. Besides, dealing with an angry man when she was in the wrong was a lot easier than dealing with one who was nice.

"I think you do." Standing up, Tristan took his cup to the sink and rinsed it out.

Karon watched his retreating back with a frown. Why was he acting like nothing had happened? The way she remembered it, she had left after an argument not after a lovefest. "I could have sworn you were mad at me."

"I was. Parts of me still are."

"Then what's with all the nice-guy stuff?"

"Don't think too hard on it, Karon. I'm this nice in all my casual relationships." With that parting shot, Tristan left the kitchen, leaving Karon staring after him with her mouth wide open.

"THAT REDHEADED TEMPER of yours is going to get you into a lot of trouble, mermaid."

Karon shot him a foul look but didn't comment. She was beyond pissed off and Tristan loved it. The phrase *kill them with kindness* was more accurate than he ever would have believed. It was sick and twisted the pleasure he was receiving from goading her, but he couldn't help it.

He was a bastard.

"Are you just going to ignore me?"

Still refusing to answer, Karon crossed her arms over her chest and stared forward. Curled up on the far side of the sofa, fresh from the shower, Karon had hardly uttered two words to him since he ran her bath.

The funny thing was, before he saw her looking like death warmed over, Tristan had still been mad. His original plan had been to come in and lay down some laws with Karon. Theirs would not be a casual relationship. Tristan had no intention of sharing her, ever. Karon was his and to hell with everything else.

But that was all before he saw her. She'd looked horrible. Some women could look great no matter what the situation was, but Karon wasn't one of them.

Karon looked like she'd been electrocuted. Her face was blotchy, eyes red and her beautiful, wavy hair had been standing on end. In a word, Karon looked like hell and no matter how angry Tristan had been, he couldn't look at the misery on her face and stay mad at her.

The need he felt to take care of her surprised even him. Yet the devil inside wouldn't let the moment pass without enjoying some part of her pain.

Reaching over, Tristan tugged on her sock, chuckling when she batted at his hand. "And after I was so nice to you."

"Why are you being so nice?"

Because it was bugging her. But Tristan knew better than to say that. So instead, he reached over, grabbed her foot again and started to massage it. Looking up at her with what he hoped was an innocent look, Tristan asked, "Why shouldn't I be?"

"Because I called you a human vibrator for starters."

What the hell? Tristan roared with laughter. "When did you call me that?"

Blushing, Karon grabbed a pillow from off the couch and held it to her chest. "Technically I didn't say you were a human vibrator, but Jacque said that I was treating you like one."

"Did she say that before the fuck-me pumps or after?"

"Before."

"Before or after the drinking?"

"Before. All the bad stuff happened before the drinking."

"So you went out drinking because you felt bad."

"I guess." When Karon shrugged her shoulders, Tristan had to do everything in his power not to laugh. She was so damn adorable.

"And that was better than calling me up and talking to me?"

"Yes."

"Why?"

Karon dropped her head down into the pillow, refusing to answer.

"Karon."

"Because I didn't know what to say." The words were muffled but Tristan was able to understand what she said. Smiling, Tristan scooted closer to her until her legs were over his lap and her bottom was touching his thigh.

Karon still hadn't looked up, but that was fine. Brushing his hand against her hair, curly and still damp from the bath, Tristan pondered how to continue. Their relationship hadn't started off on the normal foot, but that didn't make it any less real to him.

The feelings he had for Karon were very real and very deep, and Tristan couldn't imagine not spending the rest of his life with her.

"You know what? I know exactly what you need."

"What?"

"A spanking."

Karon's head shot up. "You have got to be kidding."

"Not at all." Reaching over, Tristan pulled her onto his lap. Karon's startled shout was soon lost in her giggle as he flipped her over, ass up, and landed the first of many teasing blows.

"Tristan, I'm going to kill you," Karon shrieked, her legs kicking into the couch.

"Doubt it." Tristan popped her on the ass. "This is for calling me a human vibrator."

Whack!

"This is for going out drinking without me."

Whack!

"This is for calling our relationship casual when you damn sure know it's not."

Whack! Whack!

That deserved two swats, the little brat. "This is for trying to make me jealous with Walter of all people."

Whack!

"You're evil," Karon roared, scrambling to get up.

It was a futile effort at best. Tristan was stronger, in a better position to hold her down and enjoying the feel of her across his lap. He should have known it would happen. Hell, he could have counted on it. But from the moment Karon's pelvis rocked down against his cock, Tristan had become hard.

"And you're spoiled." Tristan landed a final blow before rubbing his tingling hand on her bottom. "Are you ready to admit that we don't have a casual relationship?"

Flipping her hair to the side, Karon looked over her shoulder at him with an evil grin on her face. "Are you still on that?"

Whack!

"Fine, fine, we don't have a casual relationship," she shouted, her voice filled with humor.

"Admit now that you adore me."

"I adore you and your caveman ways."

Tristan chuckled, adding another smack to her bottom. "No ad-libbing necessary."

"Sorry."

"Liar."

Laughing, Karon pushed up, trying to rise off his lap.

"You want up?"

"Yes."

"Are you going to be a good girl?"

"Not a chance."

Tristan couldn't help but to smile as he released her. "Just what I wanted to hear."

Instead of sitting back on the couch, Karon straddled his lap. When she felt his erection, she raised a brow and rotated her hips a bit. "Pervert."

Looking down at erect nipples showing through her shirt, Tristan returned Karon's look. "I could say the same of you."

Karon got up on her knees and leaned forward, brushing her nipples across Tristan's closed mouth. "I think you should punish me some more. I've been very bad."

Crushing her to him, Tristan opened his lips and sucked in one of her hardened nipples, shirt and all. Karon's fingers wound in his hair, pressing him closer to her breasts as he took his time, teasing and stroking the bud before switching to pay the other breast equal attention.

Tristan moved his hands down her side, pushing her shorts down until they lay at her knees. Still straddling him, Karon couldn't move. His legs prevented her from closing hers and the pants prevented her from spreading her legs farther. She was at his mercy. Just the way he liked it.

"Ahhh." Karon drew in a rough breath as Tristan slid his finger across her clit. She was wet and warm, slick from her desire.

Tristan held on to her lower back with one hand while dipping his finger into her slick center with the other. It only took a few thrusts before Karon began to pump herself down on his hand. Her hips rocked back and forth, drawing his fingers inside her as though she were fucking his cock instead of his hand.

"Fuck me . . . yes . . . yes . . . " Karon cried as her fingers began to grip his shoulder blades, almost to the point of pain.

Tristan looked up to see the desire on her face. He wanted to watch her go over. He wanted to see her come. "Let go, mermaid. Come for daddy."

Tristan took his hand off her back and delivered one final well-timed blow to her ass, sending Karon screaming into her orgasm.

Her orgasm was powerful yet beautiful. Her auburn hair

looked like roaring flames around her shoulders, her face was marked with need.

God he wanted her.

The pain he felt from his restrained cock was nothing compared to the joy he felt as he continued to stroke Karon. Tristan could have stayed there all day, pleasuring Karon over and over, but his mermaid had other ideas.

Grasping his hand, Karon moaned softly as she pulled him away from trembling flesh. "No more, please. I won't be able to stand it."

"That's the idea."

Karon chuckled. Sitting down on his lap, she laid her head on his shoulder as she tried to steady herself. Taking his damp hand in hers, Karon brought it to her mouth, cleansing his fingers of her essence, one by one.

Unable to resist her sweet lips, Tristan moved forward and kissed her. Exploring her mouth, fragrant with her own juices, was one of the most erotic things Tristan had ever done. The sweet smell of her sex drifted from off her lips, enticing Tristan all the more. He had to have her.

Lifting Karon up, Tristan made her stand and pushed her shorts to the floor in one fluid motion. He had to get inside her or he would die. The need tore at his soul, so desperate was his desire for her.

Karon's desires must have matched his own because she instantly reached for his belt. Clothes flew in every direction in their haste to undress each other completely, and before he knew it, they were splayed on the pile of clothing on the floor.

There were better places to do this. A couch lay two inches

from them, yet they didn't make it that far. They moved quickly, as if in harmony with one another.

Tristan moved into Karon, thick with need. She was slick yet tight and it took a few thrusts before he was seated fully inside her. The second he entered her to the hilt, all sense of urgency left him. He was home.

Pulling out slowly, Tristan looked down into Karon's face. Her eyes were closed tightly, her lips parted as if in silent prayer. She was beautiful.

"Tell me what you want." Tristan tethered his cock inside of her. Neither pushing fully in or pulling fully out. It was torture for him, being this close to heaven, yet so far away, but he needed to hear her say the words that were rolling around inside his mind. He needed Karon to admit she was his.

"You. Please. Only you."

It wasn't enough. Tristan wanted more. "Tell me to fuck you."

"Fuck me, please," she begged, pleading for her release.

Pushing into her, Tristan couldn't resist the temptation of her body. "Tell me you're mine."

"Yours. Only yours," she growled, pulling him deeper into her body.

"Now tell me you love me."

Karon opened her eyes and met his unflinching stare. "I love you."

The words echoed in his head as did her pleas. Karon loved him. She loved him.

Tristan ground his teeth as wave after wave of lust flooded his senses. She was so fucking tight. Her body was made for him and him alone. So wet. So tight. So his.

Picking up his speed, Tristan began to power inside her harder and faster, with her words of love pushing him on. Pushing deeper and farther with every thrust.

He moved inside her for what felt like hours, keeping them both on the edge until he thought he'd go mad with the need. Karon moaned in pleasure, begging for the release. Unable to hold back any longer, Tristan reached down to rub her throbbing clit, causing her to arch upward and scream his name.

"Come for me, baby. Come for me."

Tristan felt Karon clench down on him seconds before she came again, clawing his back with her release. "Yes. Tristan. Yes."

But Karon wasn't alone in her pleasure. Tristan drove deeper within her, pumping her body until he spilled his seed into her welcoming flesh, growling out his own words of love for her.

The pleasure seemed to last forever, yet not long enough. Every nerve seemed more alive, tingling from the delicious waves of aftershock. Tristan wanted to stay inside her forever, until every last ounce of his seed flowed inside of her, marking Karon from the inside out. She was his. His woman. His heart. His everything.

"Good Lord, you should punish me more often."

"I plan on it." Pulling out of her body, Tristan rolled onto his side, still trying to catch his breath. "I meant what I said, Karon."

Turning her toward him, Karon brushed her hand across his cheek. "As did I. I think I've loved you forever."

"The feeling is more than mutual." Lying down on his back, Tristan let out a sigh of contentment. "Do you know what I was doing while you were in the shower?"

"Rifling through my panty drawer for something to wear?"

"Hardly." Tristan snorted. "I was going over your list."

Groaning, Karon dropped her head onto his shoulder. "Please don't ever mention that list again. It's nothing but trouble."

"Not even close. It enabled me to finally get the woman I've been mad about for years to notice me."

Karon rolled back over onto her side and smiled. "I noticed you. I just never figured you'd be interested in me."

"Oh, I'm interested all right, so much so that I added a few things to the list." Tristan sat up and searched for his jeans, lost somewhere underneath the pile of clothes they had made a bed out of. Finding them, he quickly dug around in the back pocket before pulling out the note triumphantly. "Found it."

Interest piqued, Karon made a grab for the list, forcing Tristan to thrust his hand back so she couldn't reach it.

"Ah, ah, ah," Tristan tsked. "First you have to promise to do it."

"Is everything on that list something you want to experience?"

Tristan laughed at Karon's choice of words. She was damn near quoting him. "Yes."

"Then it's something I want to do."

"I was hoping you'd say that." Handing Karon the paper, Tristan waited to see what her response was.

It only took Karon a second to come across his hastily written message at the bottom of her to-do list. "Are you kidding?"

"No, and remember, you can't back out."

Tears glimmered in her blue eyes as she stared at him in shock. "I can't believe that you . . ."

"I love you, Karon. I want to spend the rest of my life with you."

"Are you sure?"

If she only knew how much he couldn't wait until she wore his ring and was heavy with their child. It was the one image that he hadn't been able to shake last night as he tossed and turned in bed, madder than he'd ever been.

Karon, for him, was it. "Well, it's on my list, isn't it?"

"And the list never lies."

"Never."

"Since I already promised . . . " Karon smiled, reaching out to caress his face.

Tristan's heart warmed at her smile. "A promise is a promise."

EPILOGUE

"JACQUE HAS LOST HER FREAKING MIND and it's all your fault."

Smiling, Karon set her coffee cup down next to the magazine she had been perusing and stood up. If she had to listen to Zoya go off on Jacque's newest insane idea, she was going to need a chocolate doughnut to go with the caffeine. "What's she done now?"

Zoya paused dramatically, before continuing. "She is taking out an ad in the personals for a boy toy."

"She is not."

"No, I swear she is." Zoya sounded amused and annoyed at the same time. "I was with her when she was filling out the stupid form."

"And you let her do it?"

"Short of bodychecking her, there wasn't anything I could do. That girl has lost her mind and it's all your fault."

Karon sincerely doubted that. Jacque had been crazy when she'd met her. It was one of the many things she liked about her. "Pray tell, how is this my fault?"

"If you hadn't made your own little list and ended up living happily ever after, none of this would have happened."

Laughing, Karon shook her head. "You're so right. I should feel horrible for falling in love. Will I get kicked out of the girl-friends club for this?"

"Shut up." Zoya's laughter filled the line. "You know what I mean. I'm over the moon for you and Tristan, but there are more frogs than princes out there and I'm afraid she's going to get hurt."

"Did you try to tell her that or did you just order her not to do it?"

"Order, please, you know better than that."

Ordered, just like Karon thought. Jacque might be a free spirit but Zoya was too bossy for her own good. If anybody needed to take out an ad, it was her. "I'll call her, but Zoya, she's an adult. We'll just have to sit back and see where this takes her."

"What do we do if it takes her right to heartbreak hotel?"

"Then we'll hold her hand and eat bonbons while watching *Thelma and Louise*."

Zoya sighed loud enough to vibrate the phone. "If this ex-plodes in her face, I'm going to say I told you so."

"I would think nothing less." They were still chatting when Tristan walked into the kitchen, fresh from his shower.

"Mermaid," he whispered, brushing a kiss on her cheek before grabbing a coffee mug and pouring himself a cup.

"Babe." Holding up her index finger to signal one minute, Karon cut off Zoya in mid rant. "I have to go. We'll talk about this later."

"Okay. Give Tristan my love."

"Will do." Hanging up the phone, Karon walked over to Tristan, who was watching her with a smile. Over the last few weeks they had been in and out of each other's houses so much Karon was beginning to be confused about what was where. They both knew they were going to have to pick a house but for now, it was fun to go back and forth between both.

Stopping next to Tristan's chair, Karon brushed her hand through his hair, damp from the shower. The sweet scent of the Swiss vanilla shampoo wafted up to her as she leaned down and brushed a kiss across his forehead.

"Morning, sleepyhead." What a way to start the day. What a way to start a life.

"Morning, love." Tristan wrapped his arm around her waist, pulling her in close to him. "What did Jacque do now?"

"You don't even want to know." Laughing, Karon went to pull away but was stopped short when Tristan tugged on her hand, forcing her down onto his lap.

"Another quiz?" Eyeing the title, Tristan chuckled. "*Is he the one?* So how did I rate?"

Surprised, Karon looked down at the magazine and smiled. She hadn't even noticed the quiz. "Oh please, I don't need a magazine to tell me I have a winner." That would be one quiz she would never have to take. Closing the magazine, Karon tossed it over her shoulder before wrapping her arms around his neck, and leaned back so she could see up into his face. "I'm in love with an amazing man who loves me back. He makes my heart sing, my knees weak and he's almost crossed off everything on my sexual to-do list."

"Oh, so it's your list now?"

"It would be if it were complete."

"Almost, huh?" Tristan tightened his hold on her and frowned. "You mean I've left something out?"

Scooting his chair back, Tristan stood with a laughing Karon in his arms.

"Put me down."

"Never." Winking down at her, Tristan carried her through the house to her bedroom, where he dropped her on the bed.

"It's okay, Tristan. Not everyone is perfect," Karon teased. She knew how much pride he took in the fact that he was fulfilling her every desire, and it only made her want to egg him on that there were two fantasies that he'd yet to try out. "All I was trying to say was that it's just a shame we are only two fantasies away from a complete list."

"Silence woman." Tristan sat down next to her as he dug out the list from the drawer. Karon watched his face, wanting to see the exact moment when he saw what the two remaining items were, and the second he did, he laughed. Just as Karon knew he would.

Dropping the list back in the drawer, Tristan climbed fully onto the bed and slid over her. "I have been remiss. But I'm sure we can fix these oversights."

Wrapping her legs around his waist, Karon pushed her pelvis up teasingly against his growing erection. "I figured we could get around to them a little later. It's not like you have access to a plane or a train.

"Well." Tristan slid his hand under her shirt, cupping her breast as he feathered his thumb across her puckered nipple. "There's always the honeymoon."

"My thoughts exactly."

Virgin Seeks
Bad-Ass Boy

Ruth D. Kerce

ONE

ALICE SUTHERLAND spotted Caleb Sawyer crouched down, working on his motorcycle in the driveway, like he did most Saturday afternoons. Fascinated, she stood on her porch, watching him from across the street.

He'd moved into the neighborhood a little over a year ago, and he'd caught her eye immediately. Hell, more than that. She practically drooled whenever she saw him. Tall, built, confident—a woman's dream.

She wasn't the only one taken by his assets either. More than one beautiful woman had spent the night with him since he'd moved in. Not that she made a habit of spying, but she couldn't help noticing when a woman came from his house early in the morning, particularly if she was out watering her shrubs.

He glanced up briefly, and her heart thudded. No. She hadn't caught his attention. Just a barking dog from down the street. She thought for a moment that maybe he'd felt her watching him.

The truth about the man was undeniable. Caleb Sawyer exuded sex—wild, rough, nasty sex. Enough to fulfill any woman's darkest desires. And that assessment wasn't just in her fantasies.

One day, she'd taken a shortcut through an alley, just off their street, on her way back from a nearby park. Normally, the alley was empty, but that day she saw Caleb there with his motor-cycle, and a woman.

He had her pinned over the bike, her skirt flipped up over her butt, and was fucking her hard from behind. One hand tangled in her hair while the other curled around her hip, and he kept asking her if she liked it rough.

Alice wasn't sure what the woman had said. She'd been too turned on by the sight of Caleb and his actions to care about anything else. His leather jacket had covered his upper torso, but his jeans hung low, and his tight, firm ass had been bared to her view. So sexy!

When he'd stopped fucking and started spanking the woman, Alice had almost moaned aloud, picturing herself pinned over the motorcycle, his hand slapping *her* ass instead. When he con-tinued fucking the blonde, she imagined him thrusting his cock into her own pussy, until she screamed and came, preferably more than once.

Not wanting to completely invade his privacy—though she would have loved to see him come—she'd turned around and gone the other way, barely able to walk, her legs trembled so badly. She hadn't been able to get that image of Caleb out of her mind since.

That's when she'd known for certain that she wanted him. No man had ever affected her so strongly or made her pussy throb so hard. Caleb was just the type of man she'd been searching for . . . for her first time.

No more waiting.

After that day, she'd tried to attract his attention whenever they met at the mailbox or during block parties. He was always nice to her, and they even shared an interest in classic films, but he didn't seem to catch on to the sexual hints she kept sending him. She'd finally decided to be more direct.

Even though it was cool out today, he wore only a deep blue short-sleeved T-shirt tucked into well-worn jeans. His black boots gleamed as if he'd just polished them. The way his muscles bunched and relaxed as he moved, like some predator, made her tingle all over. She'd had many a fantasy of running her fingers through his thick brown hair, over his bare chest and down to his cock. Oh, yes.

If she was going to do this, she needed to do it now, while the opportunity existed. "Time to turn fantasy into reality," she murmured.

Taking a deep breath, she walked down the two concrete steps, along the path, over the sidewalk, paused, then crossed the street and continued up his drive. So far, so good. She gathered all her strength and forced her voice to work, hoping she sounded less nervous than she actually felt.

"Hi, Caleb."

He glanced up, then returned to fiddling with the bike. "Hey, Ali. You're home early from the library today."

She loved the way he called her Ali. No one else did, and she thought it sounded sexy. "I'm not working this weekend."

Continuing with his repairs, he grunted in response.

She knew on weekends he didn't go into the motorcycle shop he partially owned. So she'd coordinated her schedule with his to have the time available to put her plan into motion. "Can I tell you something?"

He glanced up, but only for a moment. "What?"

Her heart pounded against her ribs. *Here we go.* "I'm . . . I'm still a virgin."

At twenty-four years old, she was sick of waiting for "Mr. Right" and determined to sleep with a man who could make her toes curl and all her sexual fantasies come true. Caleb was that man.

He stopped working. He didn't look at her, but she saw his hand tighten on the wrench he held. After a moment, he continued tightening whatever he was tightening. "And?"

"And?" she repeated in confusion. That wasn't quite the response she'd expected.

"I'm assuming after a statement like that, there's an *and* attached."

The man was too smart for his own good. "Well, yes." Her stomach fluttered, and she felt a little lightheaded at the thought of his large hands stroking her breasts, her pussy, the soft skin between her thighs, her ass. She could hardly wait.

"I want you to devirgin me."

No response. He simply continued working. Hmm. Okay, this didn't bode well.

"Did you hear me?"

"I heard."

"Well?" She felt a bead of perspiration slide between her breasts.

"Forget it, Ali."

What? Forget it? Just like that. His quick answer and casual attitude not only surprised but irked her. Weren't men always on automatic or something when it came to sex? He at least could have the decency to look up and appear shocked.

Because of the different women she saw over here, she'd been so certain . . . No. She shook her head. She refused to get upset or rattled in front of him. He wasn't worth it. Not on an emotional level. She didn't even know him really. His body was the only thing she wanted. Well, maybe not only his body, but that's as much as she'd allowed herself to expect or hope for from him.

Okay, fine. He had turned her down. If the sex alone wasn't enough of a temptation, she was prepared to offer him an additional incentive. She raised her chin and made sure her voice came out sounding strong and confident. "I'll pay you."

The wrench fell from his hand, and he surged to his feet. "Excuse me?" He towered over her.

His green eyes practically burned her skin in their intensity. She backed up a step and clutched her hands together but didn't run, not about to let him intimidate her into changing her mind. "I'll pay you for one weekend of your time."

"You want to pay me to fuck—"

"Stop!" She put her hands up as if to ward off his words. As soon as the protest left her mouth, she regretted it. *Great.* Now she sounded like a prude as well as a virgin. She wasn't a prude. He'd just caught her off guard.

"Believe me, princess, you don't want a guy like me pumping away at your pussy, especially your first time. Go find yourself a nice, safe, respectable librarian."

He'd put that crudely on purpose. "I'm not a princess, and I don't want someone safe. I want wild and passionate!"

"Wild and passionate, huh?" He hesitated and then a gleam entered his eyes. "All right, lower your pants, lean over the bike and I'll fuck you right here. We'll put on a show for the neighbors." His hand brushed across his crotch.

Her gaze lowered a moment, following the movement, then snapped back to his eyes. "That's not funny."

"It wasn't meant to be. I'm into kink, baby. On the edge, hard, rough, down and dirty fucking."

She couldn't help but recall the image of him in the alley. Her pussy clenched in need. Wouldn't he be surprised if she said okay? On-the-edge sex was just what she wanted from him, after all. She almost laughed at the thought of saying so, just to see the look on his face. Instead, she shrugged. "Obviously, I want something private and tender too."

His eyes held almost a humorous look now, and one side of his mouth hitched into a half-smile. "You think I can give you all that—wild, passionate *and* tender?"

She nodded.

"Well, I'm flattered. But I'm not your guy."

"I want to have sex with you, Caleb."

His eyebrows shot up, as if he hadn't expected her to push the issue once he refused.

Appearing from the opposite side of a line of bushes, two elderly ladies strolled by. Oh, goodness! They nodded at her and Caleb as they passed. She hoped the women hadn't heard anything. She didn't want the entire neighborhood to know her business.

Caleb curled his fingers around her arm. "Let's take this conversation inside." He dragged her through his garage and into the house, slamming the back door closed behind them. He released her arm and plowed his fingers through his hair. "You can't just go around asking men to . . . to have sex with you, Ali."

"I haven't been. Yet. Only you."

His lips thinned, and a muscle in his jaw twitched. He paced, grumbled something under his breath she didn't understand, then stopped directly in front of her. But he remained in profile, staring at the wall, as if unwilling to look into her eyes.

He seemed totally uninterested in her proposal, darn it. So much for her plans. Now would be a good time to walk out on him, except he blocked her path to the back door.

His nostrils flared as he took in a deep breath then released it. Finally, he spoke. "Why come to me? I'm sure you work with plenty of men you could ask."

Not really, and she saw no reason to prolong this torture with a question-and-answer session. She supposed she'd have to resort to "Plan B" now. Despair filled her more than she'd expected. She really wanted Caleb.

"Forget it." She used his words. They were, after all, to the point. "Forget I said anything about sex at all." She turned to leave through the front.

His hand on her arm stopped her. "Wait. Look at me, Ali." His voice came out soft but firm. "Look at me," he repeated in a stronger tone when she didn't immediately meet his eyes.

CALEB'S HEART RACED. His jeans felt uncomfortably tight. He'd grown hard the moment "devirgin me" had spilled from Ali's lips—the last thing he'd expected from her. And the most erotic thing he'd heard in a long time, especially coming from such a full, pouty mouth.

Her confession had more than surprised him. He couldn't remember ever seeing her with a steady guy but never gave it much thought. Though not classically beautiful, she possessed a gorgeous mouth meant for kissing and sucking a man's dick, sparkling green eyes that drew people in, and a suppressed sexiness that he wouldn't mind seeing unleashed. She hadn't run when he'd tried to scare her away either. Impressive.

This time she met his eyes full-on. "What?"

"Why do you want to do this?" he asked, intrigued.

"Why do I want to have sex?"

He smiled indulgently. "Why do you want to have sex with me?" Somehow, the answer mattered to him, and more than he thought it should.

"I told you. Besides, you're really hot and have always been nice to me." She raised her chin a notch. "Until today. See, I thought you were probably good at sex. I notice women over here all the time."

All the time was a bit of an exaggeration, he thought, but he would like to think he was good at sex. A smile tugged at his lips. He'd never heard any complaints, nor had any problems getting a woman into bed. The fact that she thought him hot, and actually said so, was a huge turn-on to him. He couldn't imagine the courage it had taken her to approach him about taking her virginity.

He studied her a moment, suddenly wondering if she might be playing him for some reason. She was a little old to still be a

virgin. No. The anxious look in her eyes told him that this situation was indeed very real for her.

"I know you wouldn't want anything more from me, Caleb.
So things would stay uncomplicated."

He felt the frown that claimed his features. Why would she
assume that? Did he come across as that cold and self-centered?
Just *come* and go, so to speak. Okay, yeah. Maybe he had done
that, and more than once. But her thinking that that was just the
way he acted with women bothered him.

"Also . . . " she started, but then let the sentence hang.

"Yeah?" he prompted when she hesitated to continue. She
suddenly looked quite nervous. "What, Ali?"

"Well, truthfully, I want a man who can introduce me to some
darker fantasies."

His cock responded to that. Oh, yes. "Like what?" he asked,
his voice low and deep.

"Like, um, what I saw in the alley, with you and that blonde."

It took him a moment to figure out what she was talking
about. Ah, right. The alley. "You saw that? You watched?" The
idea set his heart pounding. He remembered that day, that encounter.

"Just for a minute."

The thought of her watching intrigued him. "You should have
come up and joined us." A smile crossed his face. "That would
have been a dark fantasy come true." He waited for her to be appalled or offended, but she just stood there, looking him straight
in the eye. Damn, she was sexy as hell. Ready and willing to test
out her body and apparently any type of sex he might want to
involve her in. The erotic possibilities played through his mind

until a disturbing thought struck him. "If I say no to you, do you have a second candidate in mind for your devirgin . . . ing?"

A moment passed before she answered, as if she were deciding whether to tell him or not. "Well, actually, yes. And you *did* say no."

She was right. He'd already told her to find another man. Still, his chest tightened at her answer. No telling what kind of jerk she'd picked out. Why he cared, he didn't know. But he did care. "Who?"

"Ed Morton from down the street."

"Ed Morton!" Caleb grabbed her arm. "He's married and twice your age, Ali!" No way was he letting Morton at her first.

She pulled out of his grasp. "He's divorced, and he's not that old. He just doesn't take care of himself."

"He's divorced? Since when?"

"Two months ago. He kinda came on to me at the mailbox the other day and told me everything had been finalized. He wants me to come over for dinner and videos next week. And just so you know, all the men I work with are married. So you and Ed became my top choices. Though you've always been my number one."

Her last sentence came out as a whisper, and he saw the vulnerability in her eyes. Touched by her words about him, and mortified by her words about Ed, Caleb had a hard time thinking straight.

The disturbing image of Ed Morton came to mind. That jerk jumped any woman with air in her lungs. His wife must have finally caught on. He just imagined the type of videos Ed had planned for their date, if he got Ali alone. Not film classics, for sure, unless classic porn counted. She deserved better than Ed.

Of course, she deserved better than him too, but . . . "Don't ask him, Ali," he heard himself saying almost before he realized it.

"Oh?" A hopeful gleam entered her eyes. "Does that mean you'll do it?"

Caleb shook his head. A virgin. How had he gotten himself into this? What the hell was he thinking? Stupid question. He knew what he was thinking . . . and not your normal schoolboy fantasies. He might live to regret this, but the offer to fuck her was too good to pass up. "Okay, yeah, I'll do it." At least she'd be safe with him. Morton probably wouldn't even want to use a rubber.

"Today?"

She was an eager little thing. He liked that, and so did his dick, which twitched in anticipation. "Yes, today." He raised his hand to stroke her cheek then realized he was still dirty and smelly from working on the bike. He let his hand drop. "Will you stay while I put the bike away and get cleaned up?"

Although she'd mentioned an interest in the darker side of sex, she still might come to regret not choosing a tender-touch, soft-words kind of guy. But he'd warned her. Once he got through with Ali, she would be far from the virginal woman who stood before him now.

ALICE'S PULSE RACED, and her breath caught in her throat. He wanted her to stay. *Yes.*

She nodded, unable to voice her assent aloud. She'd probably stutter like an idiot. Her fantasy, and with her fantasy lover, was about to become a reality.

"I won't be long." Caleb turned and went back into the garage.

She stood there staring toward the door, not sure what to do with herself. "I can't believe this is actually happening," she whispered, then giggled as her nerves bubbled to the surface. Good nerves, of anticipation. A few minutes later she heard the garage door come down and the back door open.

"Make yourself comfortable," Caleb called out, then disappeared into what she assumed was his bedroom.

Feeling more than a little out of place, she gingerly sat on his brown leather couch and put her hands between her knees. Finally, sex.

She hoped not to be disappointed. Though she couldn't imagine that happening with Caleb. She knew women who hated sex and others who loved it. She wanted to be in the "love it" category. She masturbated but never penetrated herself. All her touching was clitoral, and she'd never had much of a climax. With Caleb, she hoped for a highly satisfying experience. Hell, she wanted more than highly satisfying. She wanted to shake and scream out from the pleasure.

She glanced toward the window. It would be dark soon. Would he want to just get it over with or would he take her out on a date first? Her heart beat heavily in her chest. She didn't know if she could survive a date, knowing what would happen afterward.

Vaguely, she registered that his house appeared neat and a lot cleaner than she'd expected for a guy on his own. She liked that. A pleasant odor even drifted through the air—vanilla. She scooted back on the couch cushion. After a moment, she leaned her head back and closed her eyes, trying to relax as best she could.

Waiting had never been her strong suit. Waiting for sex, well, talk about stress!

Another nervous giggle threatened, but she squashed it. She wondered how she'd feel about her decision to do this after the weekend was over . . .

TWO

"Ali?"

Her eyes fluttered open. It seemed as if only a moment had passed, but she noticed the first shadows of dusk through the window. She must have fallen asleep.

Caleb stood in front of her, his hair moist from a shower. Wrapped around his waist was a deep green bath towel, the exact color of his eyes, and nothing more. Major hunk alert! His bare chest, so broad and strong, made her feel very feminine all of a sudden.

He held out his hand. "Are you ready?" He smiled slightly. "Or have you come to your senses and changed your mind?"

Tremors racked her body. She wasn't sure her legs would even support her. Sexual excitement rushed through her, making her skin tingle. "I haven't changed my mind, Caleb. I'm ready." No way was she passing up the opportunity to feel his body against hers, inside hers.

Apparently he just wanted to get on with it, which was fine with her. She liked that he had cared enough about her feelings to shower first. She slowly stood, taking his hand to steady herself.

His warm, strong fingers closed around hers, making her feel safe and secure. But when she met his gaze, the hungry look in his eyes made her feel anything but safe.

"You sure you don't want to take some time to rethink this and maybe wait for a guy who's ready to give you a commitment, Ali?"

He must have seen the nervousness in her gaze, felt the trembling in her hand, to give her yet another opportunity to run. "I'm sure. I've already spent too much time thinking and waiting." And that was the truth. Now that he'd agreed, she didn't intend to let Caleb get away from her.

"All right. Just remember, you asked for this."

The tone in his voice gave her a moment's pause and her step faltered. She wondered if his bedroom would be all leather, filled with whips and blindfolds and sex toys. He'd said he liked kink. He might have erotic art on the walls, a mirror on the ceiling, sex-enhancing drugs on hand. She swallowed hard. No telling what he was leading her into. She raised her chin, prepared to face whatever erotic experiences he had in mind for a definite night to remember.

He showed her into a dimly lit bedroom. A massive king-size bed with a mirrored headboard took up most of the room. Black covers were neatly turned down to reveal beige sheets. Green candles flickered atop the dresser. Soft music wafted in the background, barely audible. Not some dark den of lust as she'd imagined. He'd made the room romantic for her. The thoughtful gesture tugged at her heart. "Oh, Caleb."

"Is the room okay?"

He was being so nice, so gentle, that she felt like crying. "It's perfect. Thank you."

"The first time should be special."

The smile that crossed his face warmed her trembling limbs. He'd gone through more preparation than she'd expected from him. Her motorcycle-riding bad boy possessed a tender heart, just as she'd always suspected.

"I-I don't know what I'm supposed to do." The words popped out, and she suddenly wished she could take them back. They made her sound naïve, which she really wasn't, just inexperienced. She knew that planning her deflowering—geez, she hated that term—would kill the spontaneity and probably a lot of the passion, but it had been the only way to get the man she wanted.

Caleb looked into her eyes. "Do you trust me?"

She let her gaze lock with his, and she realized that she truly did trust him to give her a great sexual experience. "Yes."

"You shouldn't," he whispered.

At his warning, her pulse raced. Had she gotten in over her head here for her first time? She was trusting a man she really didn't know to take her virginity. But at the same time, she'd never felt so turned on. Yes, Caleb was worth the risk.

He pushed a stray strand of hair behind her ear. His fingers brushed her neck, and his thumb eased across her bottom lip. "May I kiss you?"

That he had asked permission surprised her and just endeared him more in her heart. She nodded and wet her lips with the tip of her tongue, grazing along the same path his thumb had taken. When his eyes darkened, her heart pounded so hard it hurt. She wondered what he was feeling. Lust? Excitement? Deep longing? She certainly felt all those things.

Caleb leaned down and brushed his lips across hers. Gently. Barely connecting. Only their mouths touched, and when he pulled back, instead of deepening the kiss as she'd expected, she moaned her disappointment.

"I love your soft moans." His hand slid around the back of her neck, holding her in place. "Let's see how many of those I can coax out of you." He glanced down her body. Her pulse raced faster and perspiration gathered under her hairline. She felt as if he saw right through her clothing.

His fingers toyed with the top button of her blouse. "I love breasts like yours, Ali. A mouthful and more. I'm going to suck your nipples until you beg me to shove my cock into your pussy and fuck you hard."

Her breath caught. The image of his mouth on her breasts and his cock inside her, torturing her with exquisite delight, almost made her come right there. "Yes," she replied, barely above a whisper.

One button at a time popped open under his fingers. She was amazed at how expertly he worked as he held her steady, his other hand still behind her neck. If she hadn't looked down, she wouldn't even have felt him undressing her.

He released her neck and stepped behind her, slowly sliding the orchid-colored long-sleeved blouse down her shoulders. His fingers skimmed her bare flesh, causing her to sigh. She was glad she'd worn her sexiest bra and panties. The pink lace against her pale skin and light-brown hair looked enticing, even to her. She hoped Caleb liked the garments.

His finger slid under one bra strap. "Pretty. Did you wear this for me?"

"Yes."

He turned her around and his fingers brushed across her lace-covered nipples.

"Oh." She felt his touch like a hot spark right through the fabric. If that small brush of her breasts affected her like no man or fantasy she'd ever experienced, she didn't know how she'd withstand the intensity of his touch when he purposely tried to arouse her.

Caleb leaned in, and his warm breath tickled her neck. He didn't kiss her, just hovered close. His nearness, and soft nuzzling, had her completely under his spell. She moaned softly.

"So sexy, Ali. I'm going to lick you all over, baby."

She practically melted at his feet. He touched the front clasp of her bra, and in the next instant, her breasts spilled out. She saw his throat work as he swallowed hard.

"Ali." He dropped the lace garment to the floor. "You're beautiful. Such sexy breasts with rosy nipples that any man would kill to suck."

She felt a blush creep up her neck. Damn. She never blushed. His words made her crazy with physical need. "Touch me, Caleb," she whispered, her tone close to pleading.

"Yes, ma'am." He smiled. "My pleasure."

She expected his hands to cover her breasts first, him to maybe tweak her nipples with his fingers. Instead, he leaned down and swiped his tongue across one hard bud. *Oh, my!* She grasped his shoulders.

"Ah, you like that."

"Yes!" The texture and moistness of his tongue dragging across her ultrasensitive nipple felt incredible and sent a thrill right down to her toes.

"Come here. I want to up the intensity level." He took her hand and led her over to the bed. He sat down and drew her into his lap, holding her close. He thumbed her moist nipple. "You're going to feel this all the way down to your cunt, baby." He leaned her back and lowered his head to suck the nipple into his mouth.

Ali's fingers clung to his hair. "Oh, Caleb." She did feel his sucking all the way down to her pussy, as if he were stimulating her clit at the same time. He was so right. The words "Fuck me, Caleb!" perched right on the tip of her tongue, ready to spill out.

He sucked and licked until she trembled and felt on the edge of something more powerful than she'd ever experienced. *Yes!* After a particularly delightful swirl of his tongue, Caleb raised his head.

No, damn it! She'd been so close to what felt like a massive orgasm. "Don't stop!"

"I decide tonight. Not you." He laid her fully on the bed then stood up and dropped his towel.

A gasp escaped her before she could stop it. Completely naked now, the whole picture of his well-toned body struck her. Caleb was indeed a woman's dream. Strong, muscular but not overly muscle-bound. Perfect. The light dusting of dark hair that covered his chest narrowed to a thin line leading down to his cock, which held her undivided attention.

Long, hard, thick. She doubted she'd be able to get her fingers completely around the shaft. The ridges and slight curve of his cock fascinated her. The purplish-red head, much larger than she'd expected, made her body flush and flooded her with desire. She couldn't help but wonder what that tip tasted like. She reached out. "I want to touch you." That impressive cock soon would be inside her—thrusting, pumping, filling her up.

"Not yet. Open your pants for me, Ali. Now."

She gulped at his near order but complied. With shaky fingers, she reached down and undid her belt, popped the button on her pants and then slowly lowered the zipper.

"Watching a woman undress always gets me hot. Faster. Show me how eager you are for my cock."

When she fumbled, her fingers not cooperating very well, he stepped forward and pulled her pants and hose off, leaving only her pink lace panties. She gasped at the abrupt move. He probably thought she was about to change her mind. Little did he know.

"There's no turning back now, Ali."

At his in-charge manner and tone of his voice, her pussy flooded with moisture and she nodded. *Oh, how I want this!*

Her mouth dropped open when he turned to fold her clothing, her blouse and bra included, and placed them on the dresser, well away from the candles. Only when she saw the small smile on his face did she realize he'd done the folding on purpose to stall . . . to drive her crazy from the waiting and to extend the anticipation.

Finally, he returned to the bed, the look on his face all serious once more. She felt so decadent, lying on the mattress almost completely naked, with him staring down at her, his eyes filled with fire, raking her body one slow inch at a time.

Caleb stretched out beside her and glided his palm over her abdomen. His fingers eased under the top band of her panties.

She gulped.

But he went no further. He stared into her eyes. "You're gorgeous. Why have you waited so long to have sex?"

Gorgeous. He sure knew how to make a woman feel good. Her clit throbbed. She needed his intimate touch. Her hips rose slightly of their own volition.

"Tell me." His fingers slid lower but not low enough to satisfy her need.

Looking deeply into his sexy, green eyes, she felt mesmerized. "I never wanted to settle, simply to have someone in my life . . . in my bed."

"Well, I am impressed by your control. Tonight it ends. I'm going to make you need sex from now on, Ali. Crave it more than you ever thought possible." He kissed her lips, and his fingers massaged the skin just above the hairline of her pussy. When she opened her mouth, his tongue entered, exploring and tasting.

Oh, yes. Her nails grazed his chest, and she felt him shudder. She liked that she could affect him physically.

His fingers teased her, moving back and forth along her skin. Caleb slid down her body and placed soft kisses between her breasts. His tongue swiped one nipple, then the other, making her arch beneath him. His hand slid down another couple of inches, and his fingers tangled in her pussy hair.

"Oh, Caleb, yes." He had the best tongue, the best touch.

He sucked a nipple into his mouth and drew hard.

Ali jerked. "Caleb! Oh!" Her hips moved, trying to force his fingers inside her pussy. When he nibbled on the hard bud in his mouth and then bit down gently, she almost lost it. "Please! I need more, Caleb. Please. Fuck me! Fuck me right now!"

He nibbled down her ribs to her stomach, causing waves of pleasure to roll through her. He licked at her navel, then lower.

Sensations exploded everywhere he touched her. If she'd known it would be this intense, she'd have approached him much sooner.

He slowly withdrew his fingers.

No! She grabbed at him.

He forced her hands to her breasts. "Play with your nipples. Pinch them."

She swallowed hard but did as he told her, sending a thrill down her body. Oh, this was so hot!

The fingers of both his hands curled inside the elastic of her panties, and he dragged them down her legs. She'd waxed her bikini line and trimmed her curls for a neat, sexy look. Now completely naked, completely vulnerable, she didn't move, hoping he liked what he saw.

He stared down at her. When he finally spoke, his voice sounded scratchy and raw. "You're staying the night, Ali. I'm going to fuck you until you can't walk."

Her whole body throbbed at his words. "I'm not going anywhere. Remember, I'm paying for the weekend."

His eyes darkened as he met her stare. "I don't want your money. I won't take it. I want you. *You* I intend to take. Over and over again until you beg me to stop."

All she managed to do was gulp and nod in response. She couldn't imagine ever wanting him to stop.

"You prepared yourself for me, didn't you?" He petted her pussy, stroking her softly. "I like that. So sexy. So silky."

Her body ached for him, for his cock. She needed penetration.

"Spread your legs, Ali. Let me inside your cunt." He leaned over and his lips came down on hers again. His tongue entered her mouth, mirroring the movement that she'd craved for so long in more intimate places. Continuing to rub and pinch her nipples, she moaned, and her legs fell open.

Caleb took immediate advantage. His finger dipped into her, and her hips jerked at the jolt of pleasure that shook her body.

He raised his head. "Easy, sweetheart. Real easy. We're just getting started."

THREE

CALEB WANTED NOTHING MORE than to fuck the hell out of Ali. He knew himself and knew he'd have a hard time holding back and not getting too rough with her. Although she seemed to get off on the idea of reckless, on-the-edge sex. "You're going to get fucked tonight, Ali, not made love to." He didn't intend to sugar-coat what she'd gotten herself into or what was about to happen to her.

"I know. That's what I want."

Damn. She was so incredibly hot, and she wanted it, was practically begging for it. He felt her limbs tremble. The look in her eyes showed determination but also wariness. Her trust in him struck hard. For the first time he could remember in ages, he felt unsure of what to do with a woman.

She curled her fingers around his upper arms. "Caleb, I want you to do it. I need you to do it."

Fuck. He felt the heavy beating of her heart. Its rhythm matched his own. "All right, Ali. But know that I'm not letting you out of this room until I'm through with you."

"O-Okay."

After brushing her lips with a gentle kiss, he slid down her body and spread her legs. Starting softly, he placed wet kisses along her thighs. She squirmed beneath his mouth and let out little sounds of frustration and pleasure.

Moving closer to her pussy, his tongue swiped at the skin along the way. The scent of her arousal filled him. He wanted to devour this woman. He glanced up at her and saw that her eyes were squeezed shut. "Open your eyes, Ali. Watch me lick your cunt, baby."

Her eyes opened, and their gazes met. She looked incredibly sexy, needy, a little vulnerable. *And all mine.* He dipped his head between her legs and licked, his tongue intimately exploring her wet, delicious cunt.

A squeal of pleasure exploded out of her. She bucked her hips, her body demanding to be sated. "Oh, yes. Please! More!"

He gave it to her. With light swipes of his tongue, he tasted every inch of her pussy. Whenever he felt her getting close to climaxing, he'd pause and let her come back down.

"Caleb, keep licking me. I want to come!"

He knew making her wait, teasing her body mercilessly, would create a more powerful orgasm in the end. "You want to come, baby? Beg me for it." His tongue lightly circled her clit, causing her body to shake.

"Oh! Ah! Please, please, Caleb."

With her on the edge, he felt incredibly powerful. Sexually in control of her. He sucked and nibbled her clit, making her crazy, making her cry out in need. Now he'd give her what she wanted.

"Caleb! Yes!" Her fingers gripped the sheets. She arched and gasped, squirming on the mattress. "Oh, oh, oh!" As he continued sucking her sensitive bud, her voice got higher and shriller. Her whole body spasmed, finally exploding in a massive climax.

Ah, yeah, baby. He'd definitely rocked her world. She would remember that orgasm for a long while. With a soft moan, she finally relaxed beneath him, and he raised his head.

While she lay recovering, he wiped his face, then dug inside the nightstand drawer. She didn't even open her eyes at the sound of him moving around, just lay there, breathing hard.

He needed to know how it felt to be gloved inside her cunt, and he couldn't wait any longer. He covered his shaft with a condom, then positioned himself. Now that she'd been sated, she might have second thoughts about continuing. He didn't intend to give her the extra time to think about it. If that made him a bastard, then so be it. Without a word, he pushed his cock into her before she could change her mind about giving up her virginity. He plunged deep, breaking through her barrier.

Ali stiffened, and her eyes flew open.

He groaned. "Oh, fuck." Tight. Hot. Wet.

She grabbed his arms, and her nails dug into his skin.

The pain barely registered. Her pussy felt too good, her internal muscles gripping him like an iron fist. After he got himself under some control, he stared down into her wide eyes. "Are you okay?" He was careful not to move, to let her get used to the feel of him inside her. It almost killed him not to plunge repeatedly into her body, but he restrained himself, trying not to become the savage, yet, that called out to his baser instincts.

• • •

AT HIS QUESTION, ALI NODDED. That's about all she could do. So many feelings and emotions flooded through her. She felt completely . . . full . . . with Caleb inside her. He was so big! And though his eyes looked caring, she recognized the banked fire behind the look.

The orgasm she'd experienced from his intimate licking had been like nothing she'd ever felt from her own hand. His entry had hurt more than she'd expected, but the pain was now slowly fading.

When she looked into his eyes, she felt a part of him. Okay, so that sounded like some silly storybook romance line, but she hadn't expected such intense emotion to accompany their physical joining.

"Ali?"

Carefully, she wrapped her legs around his hips to let him know that she still wanted him. He sank deeper inside her, and they both gasped. This time, her reaction came from pleasure, not pain. She raked her nails down his back and smiled when he shivered. This first time, with this man, she'd never forget.

"I'm okay, Caleb. You don't have to hold back." She wanted a great experience, but she really wanted him to have a great experience too. That's how she wanted him to remember her and this night, as a hot and sensual encounter.

He moved his hips forward and back, easily and slowly. His tongue traced the shell of her ear. "You're so tight, Ali. Being inside you, fucking you, feels incredible."

Oh, yes! Oh, goodness! The slight curve of his cock touched all her sensitive points when he pushed deep. She turned her head and kissed him. Their tongues touched and caressed. She tasted her own cum still lingering in his mouth. She actually enjoyed the flavor and swirled her tongue, trying to get more. Her legs tightened, and she pushed up against him.

He moaned and lowered his head to her neck, licking and kissing her heated flesh. He slowed his movements.

"Don't hold back," she repeated. "I need you. Fuck me!" The plea she heard in her own voice surprised her. But she spoke the truth. She hungered for more. More of him. More of everything.

Caleb untangled her arms from around his shoulders. He pressed her hands down to the mattress on either side of her head and wrapped his fingers around her wrists. When he raised his head, his eyes burned into hers. "You want me to take you like some animal? Is that it?"

"Yes," she breathed out raggedly, her heart rate jumping. "I do. Fuck me, Caleb. Hard."

CALEB'S BLOOD RUSHED through his veins. She wanted it. He'd give it to her. His mouth swooped down on hers, and his tongue plundered her mouth, sweeping inside, tasting, commanding, taking what he craved. And giving back what she seemed to crave in return.

He pulled away, stared into Ali's desire-filled gaze and tightened his hold on her wrists. He pushed his cock deeply into her body, withdrew, then plunged back in hard.

She gasped.

He groaned from the pure pleasure of fucking this woman. He withdrew halfway and stared into her eyes. When her lips parted to draw in a deep breath, he thrust into her again. Harder.

This time her gasp was louder, sharper.

Yeah. She did get off on being fucked hard, rough. With a growl of savage need, he pumped his hips, plunging into her like a man starved for a woman's body. For *her* body. Over and over, he thrust into her. Harder and harder. He couldn't get deep enough.

"Yes, Caleb!"

Her body spasmed around his. Her back arched, and cries of pleasure spilled from her lips. "Ohh!"

The sound of skin slapping against skin, along with her moans and heavy breathing, sent a wave of pure lust through him. When his eyes locked with hers, a deeper connection hit him than he'd ever expected. "Ali . . . " Her name tore from his lips.

Caleb released her wrists. He pinched her nipples, and she cried out again, louder, arched her back tighter. "That's right. Keep coming, baby."

"Yes!"

He pumped his hips faster, knowing she had more in her to give. Her cries of passion and the beautiful flush of sexual excitement on her body made him crave to give her as strong a climax as possible.

"I love it, Caleb! More!"

When she came a third time and screamed his name in her ecstasy, he lost it. "Oh, fuck!" A roar exploded from him as his body crested, and he toppled over the edge to join her in a climax so strong he nearly passed out.

They both lay gasping, trying to regain their breath. Finally,

Caleb rolled off her. He took care of the condom, then returned to the bed and dragged Ali against his side. "Are you okay?" His own limbs still felt shaky.

"Better than okay," she answered. Her voice sounded winded.

"Sore?"

"Not that I can feel. All I feel right now is exhausted bliss." She glanced up at him with tears in her eyes.

He sucked in a sharp breath and didn't know what to say. He caressed her back and hip. "You'll feel it in the morning. Get some sleep." Emotions roiled inside him—caring, possession, need, protectiveness. Somehow, he felt the urge to say something more, something soft and soothing, to her. "Ali?"

When she didn't answer, he glanced into her face. Sound asleep.

Thinking about their night together, he pulled away from her and walked into the bathroom. After taking a leak and cleaning himself up, he grabbed a washcloth, ran lukewarm water over the cloth, then squeezed it out. With a second, dry washcloth, he returned to the bedroom. What he couldn't put into words, he could express with at least a small amount of kindness.

Carefully, so as not to wake her, he cleaned her body. He hoped she wouldn't be too sore in the morning. The way she lay on the bed reminded him of an angel. The way she'd fucked him and begged for more was closer to pure sin.

He deposited the washcloths in the laundry basket, then returned to stretch out beside her. He drew her closer and covered them both with the sheet and blanket.

No way was he letting this woman just walk out of his life. She might have only planned to lose her virginity tonight, then go back to her everyday life without him, but he'd find some way to change her mind. He'd never come so hard with a woman, and he intended to have more than just one weekend of pleasure.

Caleb's eyes slowly opened, and he stretched languidly under the covers. He glanced toward the rays coming through the window. Normally, he hated mornings. Today, he looked forward to greeting the sun. A smile crossed his face. What a great night. He hadn't felt so content after a bout of sex in a long while. He turned onto his side, reaching for Ali at the same time.

The bed was empty.

He bolted upright. His gaze swept the room. Everything lay still and quiet. Her clothes were gone. He looked at the clock. Almost eight. Early. He plopped back down, and a wave of depression took hold.

Ali was gone. For how long, he wondered. He'd been so sated that he'd slept right through until morning.

"Well, okay, fine," he mumbled to himself, suddenly not so excited about the day after all. "It's over." She'd wanted her cherry popped. He'd done it. She'd left. Case closed. Except, damn it, he couldn't get her out of his mind and didn't want to just let her go.

He cringed, thinking how she might have allowed Ed Morton the same access to her body. She was one unique lady. She deserved the best of everything in her life. He was certainly far from the best, but somehow she made him want to be better. For her.

Fuck. He shook his head. Sex. That's all this was. Don't make the encounter into anything more, he told himself. Just because she embodied what he craved in a woman didn't mean their sleeping together might have grown into something more than physical if she'd stuck around. He admired her and had enjoyed their time together. The sex had been fantastic. But he couldn't even really call her a friend. They didn't know each other well enough.

The smell of fresh coffee caught his attention. "What the hell?" He tossed back the covers. Was it possible?

After pulling on his robe, he followed the aroma to the kitchen. Ali sat at the table.

She hadn't left him. He felt like shouting "*Yes.*"

He stepped inside the arched entry. "Um, hi." Her clothes were different. She must have gone home, changed and then came back. He liked that she came back.

Her gaze snapped up to his. "Oh, hi." She scrambled up from the table. "Would you like some coffee?"

He slid into a seat. "Please. You left?"

She shrugged. "I went home, took a bath and changed clothes. I wasn't sure you'd want me here this morning. But then I felt strange about leaving without saying anything." She set a cup of coffee in front of him. "So I came back."

"Why would you think I wouldn't want you here? We could have showered together this morning. I'd love to slide my hands over your wet body and help you wash every inch of soft skin." He wiggled his eyebrows.

"Mmm, that does sound nice." A smile tugged at her lips. "I guess I just didn't want to intrude too much on your life."

"You're the one who wanted the weekend." When she

frowned, he realized how that sounded. "And I want the weekend too. The whole weekend."

She smiled widely.

Beautiful. The fact that she'd returned and made herself comfortable in his kitchen gave him a warm feeling inside. Her presence made everything seem nicely domestic, like he lived in a real home instead of just a house. "Sit with me."

She sat across from him at the small oak table.

Suddenly wondering if another reason might exist for her leaving, concern rolled through him. "You are okay, right? I didn't hurt you last night, did I?" At one point, he'd been pretty rough with her.

"No, of course not." She reached for his hands. "You were great, Caleb. Making love with you was better than I ever imagined."

Making love—that's how she viewed it. He didn't know what to think. They'd fucked, pure and simple. But somehow . . . it did seem to be more than that.

"Thank you so much for everything."

He didn't know what to say. He cleared his throat, thinking he needed to say something profound, but came up empty. When he pulled his hands away, feeling inadequate, her smile faded and she actually looked hurt. An arrow of pain lodged in his heart.

ALI SAT LOOKING AT HER HANDS atop the table, not knowing what to say. Her body felt sated, but her emotions were one big jumble today. She'd love to explore a real relationship with Caleb, but she knew that kind of thing scared men off, so she wasn't about to say anything. They'd only spent one night together, after all. She didn't want to make him feel invaded or trapped or whatever a man felt when a woman pushed into his life too quickly.

Everything had gone great last night. She'd never forget the way he'd made her feel. She found it amazing, though, how the light of day could make things feel so unsettled.

She sighed and looked up at him, getting more confused by the moment. First, he'd tried to shoo her away, not wanting to sleep with her. Now he seemed to want her around. Had their intimacy changed him? Or was that simply wishful thinking on her part? She didn't know. She only knew that making love with him had certainly changed her.

"Ali." He smiled gently. "This weekend is for fun, so let's have fun and not worry about anything else for now." He stood up and pulled her out of the chair. "Okay?"

He'd obviously picked up on her turbulent emotions. "Okay." When he hugged her tightly, she wrapped her arms around him. She'd enjoy all the time she could with Caleb and make some lifetime memories for herself this weekend. After that, she'd deal with whatever happened.

FOUR

S DUSK SETTLED outside, casting shadows around the room, Ali plopped down on Caleb's couch, feeling content. They'd spent a wonderful day together.

Caleb tossed his keys on the coffee table, then flipped on a lamp. "Did you like the motorcycle ride?"

"I loved it." She'd felt completely free riding behind him. What a thrill! In fact, she'd felt so alive today with Caleb that returning to her old, mundane life as a librarian held little appeal.

"Thanks for taking me by the motorcycle shop. It was interesting to see where you work. The place looked bigger on the inside than it appeared from the street."

"I'm glad you liked it. We added on to the back end last year. One day I hope to solely own the shop and even expand to more cities in the area."

His eyes lit up as he spoke. She admired his passion for something he obviously loved.

"And now . . . " He tugged her to her feet. "My sexy beauty, enough about business." He cupped her cheek, stroking her skin with his thumb.

His words and touch took her breath away. Heck, just one look from him, with those "let's fuck" eyes, made her melt.

"The weekend isn't over yet. So what do you want to do? Lady's choice."

She chewed at her bottom lip a moment, then released it. She knew exactly what she wanted, and she intended to let him know too before her time with him ended. "I want to learn how to properly . . . suck your dick."

His eyes widened, and a burst of husky laughter escaped him. "Oh, fuck, yeah." He grabbed her hand. "Come on."

Caleb brought out a more sensual side of her personality than she had ever realized existed, even in her fantasies. She followed him into the bedroom, eager to continue their erotic weekend.

A thought struck her. "Um, Caleb." She tugged a moment on his hand. "Wait. You don't think I'm just all sex-crazed or some-thing, do you?" she blurted. She wanted him to think of her as more than simply a warm body in his bed. Strange, actually, con-sidering the dynamics of their relationship and what she'd origi-nally approached him for, if you could even call what they had a relationship.

He sat down on the bed and laughed. And laughed. He held his stomach.

Somehow, she didn't find this all that funny. "Caleb!" She slapped at his shoulder. "Stop already." She didn't know if he was laughing at her, what she'd said or the whole situation.

"You, Ali, are a real jewel."

"What?" A jewel? That was a good thing, right?

He pulled her down beside him. "I haven't had such fun with someone in a long while."

"Truly?" Her whole body warmed.

"Truly."

She saw the honesty of his words in his eyes and in the smile on his face. She felt much the same about him. She'd needed excitement and fun in her life, and he had filled that need. She doubted she'd ever grow tired of a man like Caleb.

Feeling secure and confident, she reached for the button on his jeans. "Show me how to suck you off."

"You bet." He pulled his shirt over his head while Ali unzipped him. With her help, he shucked his jeans and briefs. He wrapped her hand around his semihard length. "Touch my dick, Ali. All over."

She knelt down on the carpet and lightly moved her fingers over him, examining the length, breadth and ridges of him with interest. She marveled at how much pleasure this one incredible organ had given her. Taking her time, she savored the feel of him. Velvet over steel. Pure male power.

Unable to wait any longer, she leaned over and kissed the tip of his cock. When he groaned, she lightly fingered his balls, wanting to increase his pleasure as much as possible.

"Ah, yeah. Nice and gentle. Lick my dick, Ali. I want to feel your tongue sliding down my shaft."

Her tongue darted out and stroked across the wide head of his purplish-red cock, then eased down his long, thick shaft. She felt him stiffen and glanced up into his eyes.

"Again," he choked out.

She stroked him once more with the tip of her tongue, enjoying the musky taste of him. Unique.

"Lick my balls."

Slowly, she dragged her tongue down the length of his cock and back up again. Over and over. Then she glided her tongue over his balls with a light, gentle touch.

"Ah, fucking great, baby."

She'd never much liked when men called her baby. But with Caleb, the endearment made her feel special and warm inside. She experimented with different licks over his cock, paying special attention to his reactions. She found a spot on the underside of his cock, just below the head, that he seemed to like her licking the best, especially when she rapidly flicked her tongue.

"Oh, yeah, Ali. Wrap your fingers around the base now."

She curled her fingers around him. He reached down and covered her hand with his. Moving up and down his shaft, he showed her the stroking rhythm he liked.

Looking up at him, she watched him move, studied his body. Firm, with just the perfect amount of muscle everywhere. His cock seemed incredibly thick. And he knew how to use it. He'd proven such a fabulous lover. She wished this weekend could go on forever.

"Enough stroking. Suck my dick now."

Yes. That sounded decadent and so sexually delightful that she smiled. Carefully, she wrapped her lips around the tip of his cock and sucked lightly. When he caressed her head and urged her to take more of him, she sucked another wonderful inch into her mouth. Addictive—Caleb was definitely addictive. Emotionally, she was sinking, becoming more and more attached to this man who had showed her all about the physical side of love by tending just as carefully to her feelings.

"That's great, Ali. Just a little more suction. Ah, yeah. Perfect. Suck it. Yes."

Ali felt a huge sense of power and control over Caleb. While she enthusiastically sucked him, taking as much of his cock into her mouth as possible, she unbuttoned her blouse and slipped the garment off her shoulders. Her bra quickly followed. She felt sexier than she had ever imagined, kneeling, semidressed, with her breasts bared, and eating Caleb's cock.

With a disappointed-sounding groan, he gently pushed her away and helped her to her feet. "Enough, or I'm going to come."

"I wouldn't have minded." She smiled sexily and ran her tongue across her lips.

"Damn," he groaned. "You're incredible, Ali. Next time, I'm coming down your throat. And you're going to swallow every fucking drop."

Oooh, that sounded good to her.

He reached for the zipper of her pants. "Get your clothes off."

The phone on the nightstand rang. Caleb frowned. He raised his finger, indicating for her to hang on, and scooted back to answer. Because of his business, he didn't want to take the chance of missing an important call. Though he was definitely tempted just to let the damn thing ring.

"Hello. Yeah, Rick. What's up?" His partner in the motorcycle shop usually called sometime during the weekend to let him know about any news. They'd missed Rick at the shop earlier, so he hadn't gotten the latest update. The man sounded cheerful, so all must be well.

Caleb pointed to Ali's pants. She raised an eyebrow, and he made a tugging motion with his hand. She smiled and continued undressing. *Oh, yeah. Show me some skin.*

"Huh? Oh, nothing much, Rick. Just watching a beautiful woman get naked."

She hesitated and that brow arched again. Caleb grinned and blew her a kiss.

With a soft laugh, she wagged her finger at him. But she must not have minded too much because she continued taking off her clothes.

He saw the erotic possibilities with Ali and wanted to explore as much as he could with her this weekend . . . longer, if she allowed it.

"Yeah, I'm listening. Go ahead."

Naked now, Ali crawled up on the bed.

Sexy, he mouthed to her, his dick hard and ready to plunge into her wet pussy.

"How do you want me?" she whispered into his ear, then sucked his lobe into her mouth. She made a sound very close to a purr.

Caleb shuddered at her words and actions. He liked her growing boldness. "Condom," he whispered.

She raised her head and nodded. Reaching over, she grabbed a foil square off the nightstand, opened the packet and, while he watched, rolled it over his cock.

He shouldered the phone and gripped her hips. Gently, he straddled her over his shaft and thrust deep. The muscles of her pussy gripped him tightly. He practically dropped the phone from the intensity of being gloved so snuggly inside her cunt. Rick said something about an order for five motorcycles, but the man's words didn't really register.

Ali moaned. She bit her lip, keeping the sound low. Caleb gritted his teeth. Ali was so hot, fucking him with Rick listening.

"Nail her good, bud," Rick said on the other end, with a low chuckle.

"Oh, yeah. I intend to."

"Intend to what?" she asked, rotating her hips.

"Ah . . . nice move. Rick and I want to nail you good, sweetheart." When her eyes dilated, and he saw her increased interest, his pulse raced. *She wants it.* He squeezed her breast.

"Mmm." She leaned close and licked at the tender skin right below his ear. "Okay . . . both of you."

At the erotic sensation, along with her words, he growled in response. While still holding the phone, he pinched one of her nipples until she moaned. "Ride me, Ali," he ordered in a no-nonsense tone, not bothering to hide his words, or their actions, from Rick since she was obviously turned on by the idea of being with two men at the same time, even if one of them was on the other end of a phone line.

Without hesitation, she moved her hips, riding his cock with abandon, as if she'd done so a thousand times. Her fingers gripped his shoulders. "Oh, Caleb! Spank me!"

Caleb's whole body jerked at her sexy request.

"I heard that," Rick said over the phone. "Spank her, man. Hard. So I can hear it."

"It's going to sting," he told her.

"Do it, Caleb!"

He brought his palm down hard on one of her ass cheeks. Too hard? The crack sounded loud, even to his own ears.

Ali and Rick both groaned.

Since she didn't protest the swat, he continued spanking her hard and now also fast. Each slap brought him closer to losing it. "Damn, you are so sexy, Ali. And you're getting off on another man listening to us fuck, aren't you? What else turns you on?" The possibilities made his mouth water and his dick feel as hard as steel.

"I'll try anything you want, Caleb."

"Anything?" He fought for control.

She nodded. "I want it all."

"You've got a live one there, bud. Let me talk to her while you fuck her," Rick said. "We'll see what she's got in her."

Intrigued, Caleb handed Ali the phone. "Listen to him."

ALI COCKED AN EYEBROW, then took the phone and put it to her ear. She was close to coming, and her ass tingled from the spanks Caleb had given her. The idea of doing something kinky with him appealed to her newly found sense of adventure.

Caleb's fingers curled around her hips and he plunged his cock repeatedly into her pussy.

"Oh, yes!" She loved the feel of his cock thrusting deep inside her, touching all her sensitive areas.

Rick chuckled in her ear. "You like it nasty. I can tell."

"Yes," she moaned, without thinking about her response. All she could think about was the pleasure rolling through her body.

"Say 'I want it nasty, Caleb,' right now," Rick ordered her. "Go on, say it."

"I want it nasty, Caleb," she repeated, unable to stop herself. She needed this sexual intensity and the feeling of recklessness in her life, at least once.

"Oh, yeah. How nasty, baby?" Caleb asked her.

"Say, 'Fuck my ass' . . . tell him."

"Ah!"

"Say it!"

"Fuck my ass." Her voice sounded shaky, but she wanted Caleb to do it. The image in her head of his cock pushing up her asshole, her totally submitting to the act, brought her close to coming. "Fuck my ass, Caleb!"

Rick groaned into the phone. "Man, I'd love to see him pumping his cock into a luscious asshole."

Caleb immediately stopped thrusting into her pussy. His eyes grew more intense than she'd ever seen before. He lifted her off his cock and pushed her facedown onto the mattress. "You're going to get the ass-fucking of a lifetime, baby."

"Yes, yes, yes . . . " she practically wailed. Anticipation filled her. Would she even be able to take his thick cock up her ass?

His hand smacked her ass cheeks, one then the other, over and over, until she squirmed and whimpered.

"Oh, Caleb!"

He lubricated her asshole with her own cream. He pushed one and then two fingers into the tight opening to prepare her for his cock.

Her hips bucked. "Oh, damn, that feels good."

"Is he doing it?" Rick asked.

"Yes," she whimpered, loud enough for Rick to hear. "With his fingers." The feeling of Caleb's fingers stretching her hole, pumping in and out, deep then shallow, hard then soft, was a feeling she'd never even imagined before.

She heard Rick's heavy breathing over the phone . . . along with another sound. Yes. He was masturbating. Sexy!

"Tell him to shove his fat cock up your hole now," he ordered.

His harsh words caused her already pounding heart to race out of control. She glanced over her shoulder, as turned on as she was, and as she hoped Caleb was too. "Use your cock. Fuck my hole, Caleb. Now!"

"Damn, Ali!" Sweat had formed on his chest and brow, and his hands shook slightly. He spread her ass wide and pressed the head of his cock against her puckered hole. Slowly, he pressed forward until the head popped inside.

"Oh! Yes! Push your cock deeper. All the way up my ass. Do it."

Rick groaned. "I'm going to come."

Caleb pushed deeper, then pumped her ass in short, fast strokes. His fingers played with her clit. "Come for us, Ali. Come."

"Come, sexy baby," Rick groaned.

Her body spasmed, and her asshole gripped Caleb's dick hard, ripping a moan from his lips. When her pussy contracted, she screamed. A powerful orgasm shot through her.

Rick and Caleb shouted as they came at almost the same time. Their groans filled her ears, and she came again, once more milking Caleb's dick with her ass.

His body shook, and his fingers dug into her hips, holding her tightly. "Fuck, yeah!"

After what seemed like forever, she collapsed on the mattress, totally spent. Rick was quiet on the other end of the phone. Caleb lay silently across her back, until finally he shifted to the side with a grunt and hung up the phone.

His hand lightly stroked her ass, but that's as far as he moved. Feeling exhausted and unable to move, she barely managed to mumble a few words of thanks for the incredible experience. Too tired to even clean up, her eyelids gradually lowered, and she drifted off to sleep.

ALI JERKED AWAKE, not sure what had roused her. The morning light streamed through the window. The weekend was over.

Disappointment rolled over her like a suffocating wave. She'd so enjoyed her time with Caleb. She never wanted it to end. He'd shown her an incredible world of sex and had given her a greater sense of self.

When she made a move to get up, a sharp slap to her butt made her squeal. She glanced behind her. "Caleb, what are you doing?"

"Getting your attention. It took three swats to wake you. Up on your knees, Ali. I'm horny as hell from looking at you lying there naked and thinking about last night. You're getting an early morning fuck, baby."

Oh, my! He was positioned in back of her, ready to go. When she faced front, she saw his intense expression reflected in the mirrored headboard as he stared down at her body. His cock stood hard and already gloved in a condom. None too gently, he pulled her to her knees.

Her heart hammered against her ribs. One last fuck before he tossed her out? If so, she was determined to enjoy it.

With a hard plunge, he pushed his cock as deeply as he could get it into her pussy. "Oh, yeah. You're so incredibly tight. I've been thinking of getting inside your beautiful cunt since I woke up."

His words sent a delicious thrill right through her. Ali hung her head and moaned. This position made his penetration feel so powerful.

He pulled halfway out and pushed back in hard.

She thought she heard him growl, like the wild predator she'd always imagined him to be. She moaned his name, loving the way he took sexual charge.

He plunged into her hard once more, pushing deep. "You like that?" He ground his hips against her.

"Yes, Caleb." This was the bad boy in full form. Pure sex, without holding back.

"I want to hear you beg for it." He tangled the fingers of one of his hands in her hair. "Say, 'fuck me hard.' Say it, Ali." He didn't ask; he ordered, tightening his hold on her.

His eyes burned into hers, connecting in the mirror. She gulped. "Fuck me. Fuck me hard, Caleb." Words turned him on, and she wanted to turn Caleb on, big time.

He pulled halfway out and slapped her ass. "Louder." He thrust back into her.

"Oh!"

His fingers released her hair and curled around her hips. He began plunging repeatedly into her pussy. "Say it, Ali!"

Her body shook, and she felt right on the edge of coming. "Yes! Fuck me hard! Hard! Oh, yeah. Like that. Oooh, rougher. Ah, oh! Faster, Caleb! Make me come!" The words spilled from her mouth.

"Yeah!" He pumped her like some sexual savage. "You love it like this, don't you, Ali? Hard, fast, nasty."

"I—"

He spanked her ass. "You're so good, baby. Damn, I love your tight cunt."

Ali's heart felt ready to explode. She gulped in lungfuls of air. "Yes, more!"

"Yeah . . . I'll give you more." He thrust into her with powerful strokes, showing no mercy.

"Yes! Caleb!" She couldn't get enough of him. A flutter of pleasure started inside her pussy and raced through her body with an intensity and speed she'd never felt before. "Ahhhh!"

"Yeah. Come for me, Ali! Come hard."

"Ohhh!" Her world exploded, her orgasm so intense she screamed his name and felt on the verge of falling into a never-ending vortex of sexual ecstasy.

In response, Caleb roared. His body tensed, and his fingers gripped her hips almost painfully. "Yes, Ali! Yes!" He came long and hard. "Ah! Fucking incredible!"

They both collapsed on the bed, breathing heavily. Ali couldn't move, completely conquered, sexually.

After a few moments, Caleb kissed her temple.

She lay quietly for quite a while, then looked over at him. "Um, can we do it again, Caleb?"

A groan rumbled up from his throat. "Again? You're going to kill me, Ali, I swear."

She grinned. She trusted Caleb completely, with her body and with her emotions. She'd never realized the power and thrill of sex and wanted to experience it over and over again, as much as possible. But whenever she looked at Caleb, she also wanted so much more than just sex. Did he?

She supposed she'd find out soon, for as soon as she left his bed, the weekend would officially be over.

Epilogue

ALI LOOKED AROUND the large, grassy field in the middle of nowhere. "Why did we come all the way up here?" she asked Caleb, who stood securing their helmets on the motorcycle.

They'd continued to see each other after that first weekend. She wasn't exactly sure how it had all happened, or who had made the first move. Being together just seemed so natural. She looked forward to their time together each and every day. And he'd shown her a remarkable world of sexual pleasures she'd never dared to imagine.

Sometimes they stayed at his place, sometimes her place. And she'd become really close with two of his sisters, who had turned out to be avid readers, just like her. The last six months had been some of the best in her life.

Things had been a little awkward at his motorcycle shop with Rick the first time she'd stopped by for a visit after the phone sex incident. But they'd worked it out, especially after she'd found out the man was gay. She hadn't felt uncomfortable around him after that. Secretly, she thought he had a crush on Caleb, but she never mentioned her feelings.

"Isn't it beautiful up here? Peaceful?"

"Yes." She took in a big breath of clean air. The massive oak trees, probably hundreds of years old, caught her attention.

"I bought it."

"What? This field?" He'd never mentioned an interest in owning land.

"Yep. I've decided to build a house up here. I'm tired of the city. It's too hectic."

Her heart and emotions plummeted. Talk about the rug being pulled out from under a person. "Oh." He was moving away. Not to a different city, but still far enough away where they wouldn't see each other daily like now. Maybe she'd crowded him without realizing it, so he'd decided to put some space between them. "This location is quite a distance from town."

"I know, but I fell in love with the area when I saw it. I couldn't resist." He touched her arm. "Hey, what's wrong? You don't like it?"

She tried to force a smile. "It's beautiful here, Caleb. It's just that—" She'd fallen in love with him, totally and completely, and didn't want to let him go. She shrugged and held back a sniffle. She refused to cry in front of him. If this was his dream, she wasn't going to spoil his excitement. "Will you be happy living out here all alone?"

"No. But . . . I'll be happy if you live out here with me."

"What?" Her voice caught. She swallowed hard. "You want me to move out here with you?"

"More than that." He knelt in front of her and took her hand. "I want you to marry me, Ali. I love you."

Love. Her heart raced, and she could hardly think straight. Tears misted her eyes. "Oh, Caleb. Are you certain?"

"Certain that I love you? Yes. Certain that I want you to be my wife and share my life with me? Yes. Now, please don't torture me. Please say yes to me, Ali."

"Yes! Yes, I'll be your wife." Joy exploded inside her. "I love you so much, Caleb."

Caleb rose and swung her into his arms. "Yes!"

They both erupted into laughter.

Ali had known that approaching Caleb with her plan would change her life. But falling in love with him had made her happier than she'd ever believed possible. And now, as Caleb's soon-to-be wife, she knew that in life, fantasies really did come true.

He walked them out into the field. "Let me show you where the master bedroom is going to be . . ."